MARY contrived to avoid Sir Ingram for the remainder of the party, but found herself watching him much of the time, and chided herself for behaving foolishly.

That night she tossed and turned in bed. Why, she demanded angrily to herself, should this man have such an effect on her? Why did she constantly think of his smile, the way he had of lifting his eyebrows sardonically, his elegant figure, the deep yet clear tones of his voice? I ought to be more concerned about whether he is guilty of these attacks—if they *are* attacks—on Teresa. But it was of no use, for somehow, that did not matter—he could not be guilty—and his image would not be banished from her thoughts.

A CLANDESTINE AFFAIR

a novel by

Sally James

FAWCETT COVENTRY • NEW YORK

A CLANDESTINE AFFAIR

Published by Fawcett Coventry Books, a unit of CBS Publications, the Consumer Publishing Division of CBS Inc.

ISBN: 0-449-50095-0

Printed in the United States of America

First Fawcett Coventry Printing: September 1980

10 9 8 7 6 5 4 3 2 1

1

The manor house at Appleacre had been built in the years before the squirearchy had considered it more appropriate to their dignity to hide themselves away from their tenants, screened by parkland, and was set but a little distance off the main road that entered the village from the north. It was true that a pair of imposing gates were placed at the end of the short drive, but they were rarely closed, and there was no lodge with a keeper to supervise the entrance of visitors. Opposite these gates was a small, plain house built in the style of Queen Anne a century before, with a pleasant well-tended garden surrounding it. Its gate, much less imposing than the ones of the manor house, gave onto a flagged path that led in a few yards to the front door.

This door now opened and a tall, stately girl emerged, paused for a moment on the threshold to throw back a laughing remark to some unseen person within, and then stepped down onto the path. She was smiling as she trod towards the road, her simple white muslin round gown revealing the grace of her movements, unhurried yet firm. On her arm she bore a small basket, the corners of a napkin visible above the edges. It might have been some gracious chatelaine going to visit some poor dependent except that Mary Wyndham, on opening the gate into the road, crossed over this and proceeded through the manor-house gates and along that drive.

This was straight, widening into a semicircle in front of the house itself, but before Mary reached this she struck off to the right, skirting the corner of the house and making for a part of the garden that was enclosed by yew hedges, and where she knew that at this hour she would find her friend and the children.

This enclosed garden had been a bowling green once, but had long ago lost the immaculate, shaven look of such places. Now it was a sheltered playground for Caroline Grafton's two older children, and they were usually to be found there in the afternoons while their mother sat and sewed, or often, to the horror of certain elderly ladies who maintained that such laxity would be the ruin of her children, romped and played with them.

Mary passed under the archway opening onto this garden and halted, the smile on her full red lips deepening, for Caroline was seated on the grass, her skirts spread about her, making a daisy chain. The little boy, Peter, six years of age, and his sister Jane, a year younger, were vying with one another to find the daisies with the longest stems. But Jane soon saw their visitor, and with a shriek of joy ran across to fling herself onto Mary.

"Did you bwing the toffee?" she asked breathlessly, and Mary laughed, holding her basket away from the flailing small arms.

"Jane! How very impolite of you!" her mother scolded, but with a hint of laughter in her voice. "You would spoil them, Mary, dear!" she continued, rising to greet her friend.

"I did after all promise to bring them some, Caroline," Mary responded, and bent to put her basket on the grass. "Peter, Jane, here is some for each of you now. You shall have some more when your mama says you may."

Contentedly sucking their toffee, the children wandered away, and Caroline sank down onto the grass. Mary dropped down beside her and idly began to thread the daisies that were scattered about them into a chain.

"When is Arthur due to return?" she asked.

Caroline smiled. "Some time today, for his business in London was not like to occupy him above a couple of days, and he should have been able to start back this morning. He will arrive in time for dinner, no doubt, but he must be here tomorrow, for the evening party I am giving is on the following day."

"The children are all well? What of Elizabeth?" Mary asked, referring to Caroline's youngest child, a baby of scarce a year old.

"Much better. That cordial you brought her soothed her cough, and she is greatly improved. Where did you discover it?"

Mary laughed. "In an old household book that belonged, I believe, to my mother's grandmother. I was hunting in the attics one day and came across it and other papers. Some of the recipes and hints in it appeared useful, though others contained the most revolting ingredients!"

"Now, if I had happened on such a book I would most likely have tossed it aside without a second glance. You, however, make use of it! Mary, some man will discover a treasure in you! You are so competent!"

Mary disclaimed, blushing slightly. "I have no desire whatsoever to marry while my father needs me," she said quickly. "I will bring you the recipe for the cordial so that you may make it whenever it is needed."

Caroline nodded, abstractedly. She was not to be put off her favorite topic of late.

"It is astounding, you know, that we are the same age and I have three children, while you are not even married, even though you are eminently more fitted to run a household than I, and vastly prettier into the bargain!"

She put her head on one side and gazed frankly at her friend. Mary was tall, but not too much so, and she carried herself gracefully. Her figure was excellent, and she had pretty arms and shoulders, a long slender neck, and a well-shaped head shown to advantage by the coils of smooth black hair that framed her face. Her complexion was faultless, white and rose, and she had a straight nose and a wide generous mouth. Her eyes, however, were her chief beauty, wide set, large and luminous, and so dark that they might have been black like her hair. The expression in them at the moment, however, was one of acute embarrassment.

"You will make me inordinately vain," she protested.

"Fustian! Besides being beautiful, you are modest and endowed with all the qualities a man looks for in a wife. You'd be wasted on Geoffrey Knowle," she concluded, at which Mary blushed yet more fiercely.

"Caroline!" she protested, but weakly, knowing

that once her friend was well launched into this subject it would be more speedily disposed of if she refrained from arguing.

"Has he offered?" Caroline demanded.

"No," Mary replied shortly.

"But he has approached your father? Geoffrey would be incapable of conducting his love affairs in other than the approved fashion," she commented, laughing slightly. "Oh, Mary! You would be wasted on a country curate!"

"Apart from the fact that I have no wish to marry and leave my father, what other offers are likely to come my way?" Mary asked lightly.

"My dear, I know! It was tragic that your mother should have died just before your come-out, and that there has been no other opportunity. Why has your father not made a push to take you to London?"

"Doubtless he would have done so had I asked him. But I have no desire to parade myself in the marriage market with neither fortune nor grand connections to recommend me," Mary rejoined a little tartly. "I am content keeping house for him and Matthew, and I ask no more."

"Will you accept Geoffrey if he offers?"

"I have the utmost respect for Mr. Knowle, and am convinced that he will make an estimable husband," Mary said slowly, and Caroline suddenly gurgled with laughter.

"What female in her right mind considers

whether the man she loves will be *estimable!*" she exclaimed. "Oh, Mary, Mary! I do not mean that I wish you to marry a rake or a gambler, but when you fall in love I promise you that the worthiness of your lover will be the last thing that you will consider!"

"I cannot imagine the necessity of considering it," Mary remarked. "I know all the young men in the locality, and none of them has shown the slightest partiality for me. And since I am not like to meet many others, my prospects are limited."

"It's my belief they are afraid of you," Caroline suggested. "You are so *capable*. Naturally Geoffrey would appreciate that, for I understand he expects to obtain a living soon from his uncle, and you would be an asset to any parson. But could you love him?"

Mary considered this. "He is good, and kind, and of good family, though a younger son. But I have no wish to desert my father. What would he do without me?"

"You would not be so reluctant to leave for a man you loved," Caroline commented shrewdly. "Your father could be just as comfortable with an efficient housekeeper. You must confess, my dear, that he takes little heed of anything outside his books!"

Mary laughed. "I do! He is forever losing track of what he intended to do because he suddenly thinks of a new reference and must immediately look it up! I do not believe his book will ever be completed, but he is content! His income is sufficient for modest comfort, and now that Matthew has finished at Oxford he has fewer worries."

"Is Matthew enjoying being in London?" Caroline asked, realizing that it would pain Mary to be told that her father was inconsiderate and selfish to keep her immured in this small village, with no company other than what she might find at the vicarage and the manor, and small likelihood of meeting with suitable young men. Mary's lack of fortune Caroline disregarded, certain that Mary's beauty would attract men who did not need to marry for money, and convinced also that her four and twenty years would be no disadvantage to a sensible man.

Mary smiled at the mention of her brother. "I have not had a letter for some time, and the last one was a most scrappy affair," she admitted. "He was so full of all the entertainments to be found in London, and the vast number of people who had invited him to parties, that I felt positively honored that he had spared the time to write at all! I can only hope that he does not let it go to his head! His income from our uncle's legacy will not permit him to live extravagantly. I am convinced that I can count on his good sense not to get into debt, or to waste his substance by gambling, but the first few weeks in society must have an exhilarating effect."

"Arthur said that he would look for him," Caroline remarked. "He did not wish to seem interfering, of course, but he thought Matthew would not be averse to meeting an old friend from home."

"I am positive he would not!" Mary declared. "You are both of you much too good to us all!"

"Nonsense! It is entirely self-interest," Caroline laughed. "If you were not here, who would bear with my starts? And help me when I become disorganized? I know that some of the old dowagers consider me hopelessly unfitted to run a household, but if you were not here to help and encourage me they would have proof of it! Now, for this party I am giving, I must have your advice. I have made myself a new gown and I cannot decide whether lemon or pale-green ribbons would be best. I'll take the children to Betsy, and then do come and advise me!"

They spent the next hour happily discussing the latest fashions, and then Mary parted from her friend and walked slowly home. It was true that she did not particularly wish to accept an offer from Mr. Knowle, who had been living in the parish for the last three years as curate for the elderly vicar, Mr. Johnson, but she was uncertain whether this sprang from lack of feeling for him, or a reluctance to leave her father.

Caroline spoke justly when saying that Mr. Wyndham did not appear to notice anything that went on outside his study, but Mary knew that nonetheless he was very fond of her and relied enormously on her company. Barely sixteen when her mother had suddenly died, she had immediately taken the running of the household into her own hands, and had dealt competently with every domestic matter since that time. Yet however efficient a housekeeper could be found, it would not be the same for Mr. Wyndham without her companionship.

As for Mr. Knowle, Mary was certain that she did not love the young man, though she felt friendship towards him. He had been interested in Mr. Wyndham's work on the ancient Greek writers, and spent hours discussing the precise meanings of the words to be translated or the phrases to be understood. Although she did not particularly desire marriage, she knew that few enough chances of it would come her way, and when her father died her life would be very bleak. With liking and friendship to begin with, perhaps love would come after marriage, she thought. When Mr. Knowle did make his offer she ought at least to consider it very carefully.

That he would make an offer she knew. Already he had approached her father and requested in the proper form that he might pay his addresses to Mary. Mr. Wyndham had told him that it was a matter for Mary to decide, and then, casually, had informed Mary that she ought to be prepared for the forthcoming declaration. For several days, undecided, she had shrunk from meeting Mr. Knowle, but still was no nearer to a decision. Fortunately, when they had met it had been in the company of others, and she was spared an embarrassment. It could not be put off forever, though, and as she reached the gates she paused, still sunk deep in thought, but vaguely aware of the sound of carriage wheels approaching.

They came from the north, and whatever equipage it was seemed to be in desperate haste. The village street was only a few hundred yards distant, and Mary, her attention now fully engaged, hoped that the driver would slow his reckless pace to negotiate it. Appleacre was not on a post road, and since the villages further south were served by a far superior road that passed by to the east, they saw very little traffic.

The vehicle, a shabby post chaise, came into sight round a slight bend in the road and began to slow down. Mary waited for it to pass, idly wondering what brought its occupants to this part of the world, when she suddenly realized that it was halting outside her own home.

Hidden from sight, the passengers descended from the chaise, a portmanteau was quickly unstrapped, and Mary saw with astonishment her brother Matthew walk along to hand money to the postilion. The man nodded and then urged his horses on towards the village, leaving Mary confronted with the sight of her brother, burdened with the portmanteau, two band boxes, and an enormous birdcage, hastening towards his front door. At his side walked a petite, modishly attired girl who seemed to Mary's incredulous eyes to be little more than a child.

Shaking off her surprise, she started across the road and passed through the gate in their wake. The gate swung to behind her, and the click of the latch made Matthew turn round in dismay. His companion gave a little scream and clutched at his arm, causing the bird cage to sway precariously.

"Oh, he's followed us! Save me, I beg!"

"Be careful!" Matthew expostulated sharply. "You nearly upset this damned bird!"

A squawk of rage came from the cage, followed by an ear-piercing screech, so that the girl's reply was lost. Matthew, depositing his burdens on the ground, grinned amiably at her.

"Don't be a ninny! Apart from the obvious fact that it *isn't* Ingram, he has no idea where you are. Mary, how are you?" he went on, taking his sister's hand and lightly kissing her cheek.

"I am well, but a trifle bemused," Mary replied, eyeing her brother with some trepidation. Several inches taller than she was, equally darkly handsome, Matthew had a lively spirit that had in the past led him into innumerable scrapes. Usually his charm of manner had enabled him to escape severe penalties, and there had been no major disturbances while he had been at Oxford. She had begun to entertain hopes that the years had brought discretion with them, but now she wondered.

Matthew's companion had been standing back a little, watching Mary anxiously. Mary turned to her and saw that the girl was rather older than she had at first supposed, probably seventeen. She was small and slight, ethereally fair, with wide, innocent-looking blue eyes, a tip-tilted nose, rosebud mouth, and a riot of short blond curls. Her dark blue pelisse was of the latest style, and she wore an amazing confection of a straw bonnet, trimmed with an abundance of artificial flowers.

"Matthew, can you not introduce us?" Mary prompted, and Matthew grinned boyishly.

"Oh, my wits have gone a-begging, getting up at the unearthly hour Teresa insisted on! I was forgetting that you don't know Teresa. Teresa, this is my sister Mary, and this is Miss Standish, who has done me the honor of promising to marry me."

Mary merely blinked before extending her hand to Teresa.

"Do call me Mary, and if we are to be sisters,

may I not call you Teresa? But why are we standing here? Let us go indoors where we can be more comfortable. If you have traveled from London you will no doubt wish to tidy yourself."

Teresa emerged from the trance she had apparently fallen into on seeing Mary. Smiling prettily, she greeted Mary and then, as though she suddenly realized where she was, cast an apprehensive look about her and moved closer to Matthew, who had seized her luggage and was attempting to balance the birdcage on top.

"Oh yes, *pray* do let us go indoors. I cannot help feeling hideously unsafe until I am hidden from Ingram!"

"He won't know where to look for you," Matthew responded curtly. "I wish you'd get the notion out of your head that he can discover everything. Oh, thank you," he added to Mary as she retrieved the recalcitrant birdcage from his insecure grasp. "I *said* that damned bird would be a nuisance."

"Damn bird! Damn bird!" suddenly squawked the cage's occupant, and Teresa broke into a trill of laughter.

"Oh, Matthew, isn't he clever! He's heard you say that no more than half a dozen times, and he's learned it already!"

"Well, I wish he hadn't!" Matthew said with a faint blush, and an apologetic glance at Mary. She stood holding the cage up and interestedly surveying the occupant, a brightly colored parrot.

"Caroline's children would be enchanted with him," she remarked easily. "But do come inside. I'm surprised father has not come out to see what is amiss."

"If he's reading his precious Plato he won't even have heard us," Matthew replied, leading the way through the front door and depositing the luggage on the hall floor. Mary smiled reassuringly at Teresa and they followed him in, just as a startled maid appeared from the kitchen quarters to stand gaping at the unexpected visitors.

"Ah, Susan, please bring some cakes and tea into the parlor. This way, Teresa," and Mary led them into a bright parlor to the left of the front door. She was still carrying the birdcage, and she set it down with some relief on a small table near the window. Then she turned to Matthew.

"Where is father?" he asked, slightly nervously, she thought.

"In his study. But as he has apparently not heard us, I suggest you do not disturb him for the moment. While Susan prepares the tea, I will take Teresa up to my room to wash."

Teresa had seemed excessively shy of Mary during the few minutes they were apart from Matthew, and Mary did not attempt to discover from her the reason for this unheralded appearance. Let Matthew do his own explaining, she thought a trifle grimly, and confined her remarks to showing Teresa to her room and helping her to remove her bonnet and pelisse.

When they were installed in the parlor and Mary had dispensed tea, she lifted her eyebrows quizzically at her brother. Now that the moment for explanation had come, he seemed ill-at-ease, tugging unthinkingly at the folds of his intricately arranged cravat.

"I do apologize for not being ready to receive you," Mary said gently to Teresa. "No doubt Matthew's letter went astray. How long do you propose to remain?" she went on, turning to Matthew.

He looked uncomfortable. "I—I did not send a letter," he muttered. "There was no time. I'm sorry, Mary, if it inconveniences you. I—I am not certain what it is best to do next. But I knew that you would take pity on Teresa and shelter her until I can arrange to have the banns called."

"Shelter?" Mary was startled, though she contrived not to show her surprise.

"From my cousin!" Teresa interjected. "He is the most abominable man, forever telling me that I must not do things I wish to do, and trying to force me to do things I detest. I truly believe that he would have made me stay on at that horrid school in Kensington if I had not run away so often that Mrs. Bloom refused to take me back in the end!"

Mary blinked at this spate of revelations.

"Your cousin? Is he your guardian?" she enquired cautiously.

"Yes!" Teresa replied bitterly. "Papa appointed him, and he is also my trustee, and what is worse, he controls Mama's capital so that she can have merely the miserable pittance he allows!"

"And is it he you were afraid of seeing? Does he not approve of your engagement?"

"I dared not tell him!" Teresa uttered, shuddering, and casting an appealing glance towards Matthew.

"You see, Mary," Matthew contributed, thus prodded, "Sir Ingram wants to marry Teresa himself."

"And what of her mama? Does she know?"

Teresa blushed and looked down into her lap. "No. I did not dare to tell her either, for you see, she is so *terrified* of Ingram that she would tell him *everything* the moment he asked her. She can *never* stand up to him, and he is so overbearing and detestable that we decided it was safer, and better for her too, that she should not know where I am. We have eloped, you see," she concluded ingenuously.

"Well, I'm thankful Matthew had the good sense to bring you here," Mary declared, her concern as she began to disentangle the threads of this new scrape Matthew had become embroiled in tempered by relief that he had not made it worse by attempting to carry off this child, for she was little more, to Gretna Green. It appeared, too, that she was an heiress, if she had trustees.

"I knew you'd help us," Matthew said with relief. "Truly, there was nothing else to be done."

"Have you approached this Sir Ingram? What is his other name?"

"Leigh. No, I did not dare. Not that I was afraid, you understand, but for Teresa's sake."

"You see, he threatened to send me to stay with an absolutely *antiquated* aunt at Cheltenham, just because I was a few minutes late returning from a morning drive!" Teresa declared. "He means to marry me for my fortune—though I would have thought he had sufficient of his own—and he tries to discourage every man who shows any interest in me. If I even *hinted* that I had any partiality for one man, his life would be in danger, so you see I could not *possibly* have told him about Matthew!"

"Surely you exaggerate!" Mary replied, shocked at this incredible suggestion.

"You haven't met him," Matthew said darkly.

"He has already killed one man I wanted to marry!" Teresa declared.

Mary stared at her. "How is that?" she asked. "And if so, how was he allowed to get away with it?"

"Oh, he was clever enough to hide it, but I know! He made friends with Godfrey, or that is what he said, when Godfrey went to ask permission to address me. And then he took Godfrey to the most *dreadful* places, and one night he was killed. Of course Ingram pretended that he had been set on by ruffians, but he was not even scratched himself, and there was no blood on his clothes, and no one saw it happen! If his story were true, then he'd have been hurt too, because they'd *both* have been attacked. But he wasn't, and Godfrey died. I'm terrified the same thing might happen to Matthew, and that's why I begged him to bring me away."

"I know it is not the proper thing, Mary," Matthew said slowly, "but it was all I could do, truly. Mrs. Standish could not have helped, for Sir Ingram would cut off her allowance if she defied him. Apart from the business of Godfrey Delaine he is a most unreasonable man, and dominated Teresa, or tries to, in everything."

"He refuses to allow me to entertain my friends at Leigh House, in town, or at any of his country houses. And I am permitted to accept only a few invitations, and even then I have to take with me a governess!" she said in disgust. "Oh, he calls her a chaperone and a companion, but why he must insist on her when Mama is able to take me to balls and assemblies and parties, I cannot think! And she is a most disagreeable *gorgon,* for he dismissed my dear Matty, saying she was too old to control me! And she has been with me almost from the time I was born, and was Mama's governess before that!"

"How odious he sounds," Mary commented, pity for the unknown Matty surging up within her, for she had met elderly spinsters whose charges no longer needed them, and knew of the difficulties they encountered when trying to obtain a new situation.

"He is *abominable!*" Teresa shuddered. "Although I have a *vast* fortune, he will allow me only a pittance, and he sends back to the shops anything which I have bought that he does not approve of. And—and he *beats* me! Truly! Only last week when he was angry with me over some trifling purchase I had made, and I argued with him, he beat me! Then he sent me to my room and locked me in, and permitted me to have bread and water only for two days. It was mainly that which showed me that I *had* to escape. Besides," she added darkly, "there have been several attempts on my life, and, as he would inherit my fortune if I died before I married, he *must* have been responsible!"

"What in the world do you mean?" asked Mary, startled.

Teresa sighed deeply. "Once, when we were at Leigh Park, there was a thorn put under my horse's saddle, so that he would become frantic when someone mounted him. Fortunately my groom was still holding him and was able to control him while I dismounted. Another time, a shot was aimed at me when I was walking in the woods. Then there was the fence on the little bridge over the river that had been sawn through. Fortunately it was a friend of Ingram's who fell in, for he could swim and I could not."

"They could all have been accidents, I suppose," Mary said, but doubtfully.

"Possibly. But not the saddle girth that had been cut almost through. Luckily my groom is conscientious and discovered it in time."

"It sounds incredible," Mary said slowly. "If your mother is unable to help, is there no other relative who might be appealed to? I know little about such things, but are there not normally two or three trustees? Could they not help?"

"The other one is an elderly uncle, but he leaves everything to Ingram. He suffers from gout and spends all his time in the country, so that he cannot see what happens. But even if he *were* in London, I have no doubt that Ingram would contrive so that he agreed with him!"

"Well, we must think what to do," Mary said with sudden decision. She had listened to Teresa's outpourings with some skepticism at first, but as the catalogue of the unknown Sir Ingram's offences grew, she concluded that even if she allowed for some exaggeration natural in the circumstances, Teresa's guardian did seem to be an undesirable person to exercise such control over her.

"Then you'll help us! I knew you'd do it! I told you it would serve best to come here, Teresa! Mary's a great gun!" Matthew exclaimed. "You can stay with Mary while the banns are called, and I will go back to town to throw him off the scent. Then we shall be married and there will be nothing he can do to harm you."

"We must discuss this," Mary said firmly. "I am not convinced that it is possible, for Teresa is not of age. You must ask Father. But Teresa is welcome to remain here while we talk things over. I will go and help Susan prepare a room."

She smiled comfortingly at Teresa and rose. As she moved towards the door it opened and Susan entered, looking rather flustered. Looming large behind her in the doorway was a tall man, even taller than Matthew, and with broad shoulders made even broader by the many-caped greatcoat he wore. His eyes were a startling blue in a face deeply bronzed by the sun, and his sardonic glance as he took in the scene presented to his gaze was accentuated by the upward slant of his black eyebrows.

"Oh, Miss Mary, the gentleman wanted to see Mr. Matthew," Susan gasped, and then, recalling her training, "Sir Ingram Leigh, miss."

Mary stared at him, encountering his gaze and seeing something there which sent shivers down her spine. She was incapable of moving, for her legs appeared to have been turned to water, and for a fleeting moment thought that Teresa was wise to be afraid of him. Then she became dimly aware of the commotion behind her as Matthew leapt from his chair, oversetting it in the process, while Teresa screamed and the parrot, tired of his long silence, celebrated the excitement by emitting a piercing shriek, then gabbling "Damn bird! Damn bird!" continuously at the top of his voice.

2

"*Your self-condemnation* at least has the merit of accuracy," the newcomer remarked coolly and walked across to the birdcage, shrugging himself out of his greatcoat and draping it over the parrot, effectively bringing its monologue to an abrupt halt. "It's all of a piece that you so foolishly burden yourself at such a time," he went on, eyeing Teresa with scornful amusement. "As for you, Mr. Wyndham, I would advise that next time you attempt an abduction, you refrain from abducting a parrot as well. They are even less manageable than foolish chits like Teresa. Get your things, child. You are driving back to town with me this instant."

"No, I will do nothing of the sort!" Teresa gasped.

"How the devil did you know where to find us?" Matthew demanded, while at the same moment Mary, recovering from her numbness, spoke too.

"Do I understand that you are Sir Ingram Leigh?" she asked coldly.

Ignoring the other two, Sir Ingram turned to her.

"You are correctly informed, ma'am. From the resemblance I detect between you and Mr. Wyndham, I take it that you are some connection of his?"

"I am his sister and this is my father's house. May I ask by whose leave you march in here, insulting my brother and issuing orders to my guests?"

His eyes narrowed, and for a horrified moment Mary had the impression that he was about to annihilate her. Then, after subjecting her to a close scrutiny, his lips twitched slightly. He smiled and held out his hand, stepping close to Mary so that she could not refuse to take it without appearing as uncivil as he had been.

"Forgive me, Miss Wyndham. No insult was intended to you. As to rights, I am Teresa's guardian and have the duty of protecting her from fortune hunters."

"If you are implying that I want to marry Teresa for her money, then you are out by a long chalk!"

Matthew interposed hotly. "I had far rather she had none! Then it would be simpler!"

"I doubt if Teresa would agree with you," Sir Ingram responded conversationally. "Would you care to be a pauper, Teresa?"

"Oh, no, that would be horrid above all things," Teresa replied candidly. "But you need not think I am coming with you, for I am not!"

"We shall see," he replied grimly.

"You cannot force me now! I have friends to help me. Mary has promised to protect me from you! You will not allow him to cozen you with false promises, will you?" she demanded, turning anxious eyes towards Mary, who found herself blushing as she saw Sir Ingram glance at her sardonically.

"No one shall remove you from here without your consent," she said firmly. "Sir Ingram, it appears that there is much to discuss. Will you take a cup of tea?"

Susan had disappeared as soon as she had announced the visitor, and while Mary waited for her to bring an extra cup and a fresh pot of tea, she attempted to make polite conversation with Sir Ingram, inwardly marveling that she could remain so calm in such fantastic circumstances. Matthew and Teresa were of no assistance, having retreated to chairs as far away from Sir Ingram as the room permitted. He seated himself near to the table where Mary had resumed her seat behind the tea tray, and responded coolly but politely to her conversational gambits.

The tea came, was dispensed, and Mary cast around desperately for a way of opening the impossible subject. Her first impressions of Sir Ingram had been of an overpoweringly vital personality, and his actions had reinforced this view. She was half convinced that, whether or not he had treated Teresa in the way she had described, he would be fully capable of such behavior. Even—and Mary shivered at the thought—to the extent of disposing of someone he found a hindrance to his plans.

She considered him with a frank gaze. She estimated him to be in his early thirties, and he had the air of command, even arrogance, that went with great wealth. Obviously a man used to obtaining his own way. He was handsome in a rugged fashion, with a broad brow over which errant black curls tended to fall, and regular features, the most noticeable of which was a firm, square chin. He was attired in a close-fitting coat of blue superfine and, though slim, was very muscular. A signet ring and a matching diamond pin in his cravat were the only adornments he wore, but Mary recognized the height of excellence in his tailoring. Teresa's fashionable air had affected her not at all, but suddenly she felt dowdy and countrified in the simple muslin gown that had pleased her until now.

"Do I look like Bluebeard?" Sir Ingram suddenly queried, and Mary blushed in confusion.

"I—I beg your pardon," she stammered, angry at herself for apologizing and yet incapable of not doing so. "I find it all so incredible."

"You won't when you know Teresa better," he rejoined.

"How can she if you persist in this plan of removing me?" Teresa demanded from her corner.

"Ah! A flush hit, my dear cousin! How indeed? But do not read undue significance into my words, for remove you I fully intend to do."

"I am going to marry Matthew!"

"Indeed? I wonder if he is fully aware of the colossal task he proposes to undertake. Let me see, Mr. Wyndham, it is precisely three weeks and two days since you first encountered Teresa, is it not?"

"About that, sir," Matthew agreed reluctantly, but Teresa flung herself into the fray again.

"It does not take five minutes to recognize the person you love," she declared fiercely.

"How truly you speak," Sir Ingram agreed amiably, casting a swift glance at Mary. "Unfortunately your acts of recognition seem to occur with tedious regularity. Over these past six months you have paraded your unswerving devotion to at least ten young gentlemen."

"They were not like Matthew," Teresa responded without any trace of discomfort.

"No, for they did not attempt to abduct you."

"I must ask you to take that back, Sir Ingram! My intentions towards Teresa are entirely honorable! I did not abduct her, and consider you offensive to say it!"

"But that is what the law would say."

Matthew blenched slightly. "You would not enjoy such a scandal," he said, but with ill-concealed dismay in his voice.

"I should not enjoy it, but I do not shrink from necessary tasks merely because they are unpleasant. Like taking charge of my dear cousin."

"We were eloping," Teresa contributed, "and if you do take Matthew to court about it I will never, ever, speak to you again!"

"You almost tempt me," Sir Ingram replied gravely. "However, since no harm is done and you are about to be returned to my care, I do not think it need come to a suit. After all, the scandal might harm your chances of making a good marriage."

"There is no need to be offensive to my brother," Mary said swiftly. "I am well aware that from your viewpoint Matthew cannot be an appropriate match for your cousin, but we are of good family and fit to mate with anyone!"

Sir Ingram turned to her and looked at her steadily, so that she had great difficulty in holding her own gaze still.

"I do not question that," he said at length. "I am not thinking of worldly considerations, merely what would be best for Teresa. Estimable as Mr. Wyndham no doubt is, if he can be bamboozled into such escapades by Teresa he is by no means the man capable of controlling her. In addition, if he is not man enough to come to me, her guardian, and plead his cause, would you expect me to regard him with favor?"

Matthew, unable to excuse himself without appearing to throw the blame onto Teresa, looked unhappily at Mary. She smiled comfortingly.

"From the little I have heard I collect that your reputation is enough to terrify anyone rash enough to love Teresa," she said tartly. "But, as you are here, the whole matter can be discussed calmly. However, we dine unfashionably early in the country and dinner will be ready in little more than half an hour. I will not permit my father's comfort to be sacrificed to this imbroglio, so I suggest, Sir Ingram, that you dine with us, and we can discuss everything afterwards when we have all had the opportunity of recovering from the shock and are more rational."

"I would have thought there is little to discuss. I intend removing Teresa from here with no more ado, having thanked you for your hospitality. We do not wish to impose on you any further."

"It is far too late for you to reach London tonight, and even were Teresa not tired after her journey and unwilling to accompany you, I could not allow her to set out."

He raised his eyebrows slightly at the determined tone of Mary's voice, and then gave her a slow, lazy smile.

"My cousin has found a doughty champion," he said softly. "What do you propose after dinner, when we will have reached no conclusion?"

"I am not so inflexible as to prejudge the results," Mary retorted. "I would offer you accommodation, but we have no more spare rooms. There is a good though modest inn in the village, where I suggest you obtain a room for the night. I will take care of Teresa, and it will be time in the morning for any plans we might make to be put into action."

"Leaving your brother free to make an abortive attempt to reach the border by setting out tonight? Or possibly France, since we are so near the coast?"

"My brother will do no such thing!" Mary said hotly. "I give you my word on that. In fact, I think it would be advisable for him to stay at the inn too!"

"I can't," Matthew said slowly. "I've shot my bolt," he explained uncomfortably as Mary turned towards him. "It took all my ready to hire a chaise as far as here, and until quarter day I'm pockets-to-mend."

Sir Ingram gave a shout of laughter and sat

back in his chair, legs negligently crossed, eyeing Matthew with amusement.

"I must hand it to you, eloping with no money! Did you spend too much on a special license?"

"Special license? I did not buy that!"

Sir Ingram's amusement deepened. "So you were proposing to sit here for three weeks, waiting for banns to be called, trusting that I would not find you? There is a greater certainty that I would discover you than that Teresa would remain constant for so long!"

"Well, you *have* discovered us," Matthew said ungraciously.

"There was no choice, I *made* him come," Teresa contributed, oblivious of Matthew's scowl. "And I had money. At least—" She hesitated, a thought striking her. "Oh, dear, I had forgot!"

"Left your purse at home?" Sir Ingram enquired amiably.

"Of course not!" she answered indignantly. "It's just that yesterday I saw the most delightful dress at Madame Blanche's, and she would not make me one like it until I had paid some of the money I owed her, and so I had to. I forgot about needing some for our elopement."

Mary began to feel thoroughly exasperated with all three of them.

"Sir Ingram, will you dine here?" she asked abruptly. "I must give cook orders."

"Without wishing to be ungracious, Miss Wyndham, I appear to have no alternative! You have spiked my guns so far, and I would be delighted to dine with you," he added, as Susan again appeared at the door to announce yet another visitor.

"Mr. Knowle, miss," she said to Mary, who turned to greet the newcomer with an abstracted air.

Mr. Knowle was tall and broad shouldered, with finely molded, regular features and carefully brushed fair hair. His sober garb and modest stock showed his good looks to advantage, but Mary found herself thinking that he did not present nearly so imposing a presence as Sir Ingram, who had stood in the doorway so short a time before.

"I beg your pardon, Miss Wyndham, I was unaware that you had visitors. Ah, Matthew, good afternoon, I thought you were in London. I will return in the morning, if it will be more convenient, Miss Wyndham?"

"Hello, Geoffrey," Matthew greeted him without enthusiasm. "Why don't you join the happy gathering?"

Mr. Knowle glanced at him and smiled deprecatingly. "I have no desire to discommode you. My business is private, and as I was passing I merely dropped in to ask your sister whether she could spare me some time. Possibly tomorrow morning?" He turned to Mary, but before she could reply, her father, having in one of his less abstracted moments heard the doorbell, came to see who the visitor was.

The elder Mr. Wyndham was tall, but now bent with years of study, and very thin. His sparse hair was white and his skin pale, for he seldom ventured out of doors. His expression was kindly, and he now beamed shortsightedly round the company.

"Why, Geoffrey, dear lad, I thought it might be you. And Matthew! Bless my soul, when did you arrive? I haven't seen you before and forgot it, have I? My memory is going, I fear." He peered up at Sir Ingram, who had risen to his feet and now, tall as Mr. Wyndham had been, towered above him. "I don't think we have met, have we, sir? And a young lady. My dear, I do apologize. I did not see you in that dark corner. Mary, you should have told me we had visitors. They will think me remiss in not greeting them."

"Miss Teresa Standish, Father, and her cousin, Sir Ingram Leigh." Mary performed the introductions briefly, not attempting to explain the reason for their presence. "They are dining with us and Teresa is staying here for a while," she added, casting a defiant look at Sir Ingram.

He merely grinned, and she felt foolishly belligerent, but she had no time to dwell on this.

"Leigh? I know the name. Haven't you a place in Kent?"

"Yes, sir, I have."

"Then I believe I knew your father. He was with me at Oxford. Sir Edward?"

"That was his name. He died ten years or so back."

"Oh dear, my poor friend. But I'm very pleased to meet you, Sir Ingram. You are dining with us, you say? Geoffrey, you must stay too. Mary, my dear, perhaps you had better tell cook. This will be a pleasant change, to have an impromptu party!"

Thankfully Mary escaped, not heeding Mr. Knowle's expostulations. He always demurred when unexpectedly invited to share a meal, but as frequently succumbed to Mr. Wyndham's persuasions. She went to the kitchen, hoping that cook and Susan, having been belatedly warned of two extra people for dinner, could provide enough for yet two more.

Having been reassured by cook, who prided herself on her good management and resourcefulness, Mary returned to the parlor to take Teresa upstairs to change her gown. Sir Ingram excused himself at the same time, saying that he would give instructions to his postilion to go on to the inn in the village, and Matthew was left to face his father, wondering uneasily how he would receive the news of his escapade.

He need not have been concerned, for Mr. Wyndham immediately demanded Mr. Knowle's opinion on the alternative merits of translating an obscure phrase literally or with a more modern symbolism. They were engrossed in this for some time until Mr. Knowle, who had been casting it suspicious glances from time to time, suddenly inquired what a greatcoat was doing in such an odd place.

"Oh, it's Teresa's parrot," Matthew replied, and went to remove the concealing coat.

Released from its dark solitude, the bird seemed lively.

"Damn bird, dandy, damn bird, dandy," he repeated in a singsong voice, until Matthew hastily covered him up again.

Mr. Knowle frowned. "Not the most attractive of creatures," he commented. "And it seems that they invariably learn language unsuitable for feminine ears from the sailors who bring them back from foreign lands! Is it possible to get them to forget such phrases?"

"How should I know?" Matthew replied, irritated. "I've only seen the damn bird a couple of times before today!"

"Tut, tut," Mr. Knowle said playfully. "The—er—bird appears to be a quick learner!"

Matthew eyed Mr. Knowle resentfully, but as Sir Ingram then came back into the room, the topic was abandoned. Mr. Knowle, considering it part of a clergyman's duty to know all he could about his parishioners, subjected Matthew and

Sir Ingram to detailed questioning, which drove Matthew to castigate him silently as a prosy old woman, while giving surly, uninformative replies. Sir Ingram, refraining out of courtesy to his host from administering the crashing set-down he considered Mr. Knowle deserved, nevertheless contrived to intimate to him that his questions were ill-bred and superfluous.

Mr. Knowle, frustrated in his laudable desire to follow the path of duty, and in addition aware of his own consequence as the son, albeit the younger one, of a well-born family, was at a loss how to deal with Sir Ingram, and lapsed into a gloomy silence. Mr. Wyndham, sublimely unconscious of the undercurrents, found himself telling his guest all about his work, and immensely enjoyed answering the intelligent questions he was asked.

"Your father would have made an excellent scholar," he said in reminiscent mood. "Of the three of us that were friends, only Anthony Drake became a don. Your father had his estates to care for, and I met Hester and was content."

Dinner was announced, and despite Mary's misgivings proved an excellent meal. To the roast beef, fowls, and tarts that had been planned had been added a cold ham, some pies that had been prepared for the following day, and some fish intended for breakfast. Supplemented with dishes of green peas, hastily gathered by Susan, and salads, and followed by a syllabub and a great bowl of strawberries, it was a meal to satisfy.

Sir Ingram devoted himself to entertaining Mary, and she found herself greatly enjoying his easy conversation. Was he truly the ogre that Teresa claimed, she wondered, or had the girl exaggerated too much? Unaware that she was revealing a great deal about her situation and way of life, she was drawn out skillfully by means of leading remarks and adroit comments. By the end of the meal Sir Ingram knew all about Mary's uncomplaining acceptance of the task of housekeeping for her father, and drew his own conclusions about Matthew's character.

Mr. Knowle, placed disadvantageously on the other side of Sir Ingram, directed most of his conversation to Mr. Wyndham at the head of the table, leaving Matthew and Teresa free to exchange low remarks. There were few of these, however, for Matthew was gloomily blaming himself for the failure of their plans, and Teresa was too conscious of her cousin sitting on the other side of the table to utter much more than monosyllables.

At last Teresa and Mary withdrew, and Mary led the way into the parlor.

"Well, my dear, we have come through that pretty well, I think," she said with a sigh of relief. "Now, what do you wish to do? Your cousin does not seem the tyrant you described."

"Oh, no, he is clever and able to exercise his charm in company," the girl replied bitterly. "I saw that he was out to enslave you too! He has a way with women, except me, for I know him too well to be taken in by his flummery!"

"I dare say, and I must believe what you tell me, but I find it hard to think him a murderer."

"He will let nothing stop him from gaining his own way. What am I to do? I will *kill* myself rather than go back with him!"

"Oh, that is a little extreme, surely? It is impossible for you to marry Matthew now, and I must confess that with both of you so lacking in money, that plan would not be feasible. We must attempt to persuade him to allow Matthew to see you in town, and hope that it will all turn out for the best."

"He won't permit it. I know that he'll send me to stay with Great Aunt Hermione. And if we were married, Ingram would have to give me a sensible allowance, so money does not matter. Now he'll banish me and keep me away from London until I agree to marry him, while he is entertaining himself with his mistresses!"

"Teresa!" Mary was not shocked at the fact that Sir Ingram should have mistresses, for she was aware that many men did so, even in the plural, but she was startled to hear this child speak of the situation so frankly, especially as, according to her, Sir Ingram intended to marry her.

"Oh, he has several," Teresa said, misunderstanding. "I saw him once, driving with one of them. 'A prime bit of Haymarket-ware,' Godfrey called her. He was with me and explained who she was," she added calmly, and Mary began to wonder how fitting a suitor this Godfrey Delaine had been.

"What of your mama?" she asked gently. "Could she not help you? Surely Sir Ingram does not have control over her income, even if he does over her capital?"

"Yes, he does, for Papa made a monstrous will leaving it all in his hands! Papa died two years ago, and I think he had always regarded Ingram as a son, although when Ingram's father died, ten years ago, Ingram was about three-and-twenty and did not need Papa to advise him. And it is Mama who was Ingram's father's sister," she concluded indignantly and breathlessly.

"Do you both live with him?" Mary asked.

"Yes, for what he allows Mama will not provide her with a house of her own. He says that she is a bad manager, which may be true, for Mama never knows what she has spent or how much anything costs, and I dare say would be shockingly tricked, but that still does not give him the right to treat her so abominably. And he also maintains that he must control me! It is beyond bearing, and if he forces me to go back I shall just run away again! Please may I not stay with you? I like it so much here."

"Well, if he is your guardian, you must obey him, I suppose, but I will try and persuade him to permit you to stay here for a while. Though I doubt he will allow it if Matthew remains here too," she warned.

"Naturally I want to be with him, but I would do *anything* to escape from Ingram, apart from going to Cheltenham, that is!"

"Cheltenham would be livelier than Appleacre," Mary said, smiling. "We don't have assemblies and there are very few parties. I think you would find it excessively dull after a short time."

Teresa declared that she enjoyed country life, and began making plans for having her horse sent down so that she could ride with Mary. Consequently she was in a tolerably cheerful frame of mind when the men joined them. Soon the tea tray appeared, and when Mr. Knowle, saying that he had to take an early service the following day, rose to depart, Sir Ingram did the same.

"I will walk with you to the village, if you will be so good as to give me your company and direct me to the inn," he said easily, and Mr. Knowle inclined his head stiffly.

Mary bade them farewell, and Mr. Knowle contrived to say to her in a low voice that he would come again in the morning, when he hoped to obtain a word with her in private on a very important matter. Abstractedly she smiled at him, and then gave her hand to Sir Ingram, who bowed elegantly over it.

"My thanks for your hospitality, Miss Wyndham. Do not allow my cousin to make a nuisance of herself. I will deal with her if she is naughty."

They were gone, and Mr. Wyndham, incurious as to why his son had unexpectedly arrived home with these unknown guests, murmured that he had some ideas to write down before he forgot them, and drifted towards his study. Mary then firmly sent Teresa to bed, saying that she looked fagged to death, and, when Matthew would also have retired, compelled him inexorably back into the parlor.

"Damn bird, dandy, dandy, dandy," the parrot greeted them, his covering greatcoat having disappeared with Sir Ingram.

"Oh, can't we find a cover for the—wretched bird!" Matthew exclaimed in disgust.

Mary searched for a piece of cloth and threw it over the cage.

"I wonder who the dandy is?" she asked with a laugh. "Not Sir Ingram, surely?"

"Rodney Morris, I should think," Matthew returned shortly. "Mary, what am I to do?"

"First I must know who Rodney Morris is," she protested, laughing.

"Oh, just some fellow who's forever hanging

about Teresa's mama. I expect Ingram has described him as a dandy and the bird has picked it up. But that's not important!"

"No, but I was intrigued. It was just one more part of this whole mad escapade. Matthew, how *could* you do such a thing? Not just elope, which is bad enough and like to give rise to scandal, but to do it in such a mutton-headed way, with no money, and making it perfectly plain where you would be!"

"There was no other way," Matthew insisted. "He does treat Teresa in a most abominable way, and she begged me to save her. If you had seen her, Mary, prostrated with fear, you could not have left her to his vengeance! As for money, she said that she had plenty. How was I to know that she would spend it? But she's so innocent like that, she needs caring for."

"Are you the right man to do it?" Mary asked bluntly. "She's seventeen, and you are only a little older, at twenty-one. Can you make each other happy?"

"We love each other," he said simply.

"That may be, but she is wealthy and we are not. You know what people will say. While I maintain that the Wyndhams are fit to marry anyone, would it be a wise marriage? They do not seem to be our sort, for I understand that they move in the highest society. Might not Teresa resent it, later, if she feels that she has married beneath her?"

"She is not so mean-spirited! And we are as good as the Leighs. Why, Sir Ingram's father was Papa's friend at Oxford. And Teresa's father made his money in trade with the Indies. *He* was not well born, but her mama was permitted to marry him!"

"You are young. Do consider it well," Mary replied, and then fondly kissed him good night.

3

Early the next morning Mary was busy in the garden gathering peas and wondering how she could help Teresa. She had completely forgotten that she ought to be preparing for a visit from Mr. Knowle, as she went over and over the information that Teresa and Matthew had poured out to her the previous day and tried to reconcile it with the largely favorable impression Sir Ingram had made on her. He could be hard, she thought, and most likely had been on his best behavior while her guest, but would he really beat Teresa, and even make attempts on her life as she maintained he had done, and as Teresa was so terrified he would do again because of her defiance? She envisaged him attacking a trusting friend in some dark alleyway, beating him to death, merely to prevent approaches being made to his cousin, and could not believe her imaginings.

Did he wish to marry Teresa, as she insisted? There was certainly nothing loverlike in his attitude towards her. Indeed, he treated her rather as if she were a naughty child. It must be her money. Mary was not stupid, and although she had known of many love matches, those of her parents and her friend Caroline, for instance, she was well aware that there were many marriages where the preferences of the parties involved were of no account. It was the distaste she felt for such arrangements that was preventing her from coming to a decision about Mr. Knowle. Yet from what her father had said at breakfast when he had been reminiscing about his friends at Oxford, Sir Ingram's father had been very rich. Could Sir Ingram have dissipated his inheritance, possibly with the help of his mistresses, and for that reason wish to secure Teresa's fortune? Surely, with the attractions she had been so conscious of the evening before, he could have secured a more willing bride if he had needed to marry for money. Teresa was not the only heiress, but even if she had been, could he be so desperate as to murder a rival?

She shivered as she thought that Matthew might

have put himself in an exceedingly dangerous situation, and a low laugh from behind her caused her to swing round in surprise, dropping her basket and scattering the pods in all directions.

"Surely you cannot be cold on such a fine morning? Or is it your thoughts that cause you to tremble? Has Teresa been painting me as the wicked cousin, merciless towards her and all her friends?"

Mary blushed at the accuracy of his observation, and to cover it she stooped and began to pick up the pea pods.

"I did not hear you and was startled," she said crossly.

His voice came close again, breathed into her ear.

"And it is my fault that these were spilled. May I help you and be restored to favor?"

She glanced up to find him half kneeling beside her, his eyes looking into hers from a mere few inches away, a mocking gleam in them. Then he smiled and turned to the task of picking up the pods while Mary recalled Teresa's comment that he had a way with women. She was quiveringly aware of his charm, and told herself firmly that she must not be influenced by it.

At last the peas were all in the basket once more, and Mary smiled briefly.

"Thank you. I will take these to cook. Would you prefer to come inside or sit in the rose arbor?"

"The rose arbor sounds delightful—a more appropriate setting for a fair maiden than a row of peasticks!"

Mary frowned. He was not going to get round her with false compliments. She indicated the direction with a wave of her hand.

"It is beyond the black-currant bushes. I will be back in a moment."

When she returned, he was standing near the stone seat, and had taken off his coat and folded it to make a cushion. He turned and smiled at her.

"Let us sit down, Miss Wyndham. I collect that we have much to discuss."

With some reluctance, for they had necessarily to sit close together on the folded coat, Mary obeyed. Wondering how best to introduce the topic uppermost in her mind, she was startled to hear him laugh again, a low, musical laugh.

"You really must not marry that tedious curate," he murmured softly.

Mary's eyes flew to his face, and she opened her mouth to reply, but no words came.

"He would not do for you, any more than Teresa is the right wife for Matthew," he went on unperturbed. "Both would be ill-assorted matches."

"Who told you that I was? But I'm not—that is, he hasn't asked me," she stammered, her cheeks rosy with mortification.

"I had the pleasure, or should I say privilege,

of walking home with Mr. Knowle last night," he said smoothly. "He contrived—oh, most politely, I do assure you—to warn me off what he deemed were his preserves !"

"Oh, this is monstrous!" Mary exclaimed, uncertain of whether to be more angry with him or with Mr. Knowle.

"What else was the poor man to think I was here for? He did not know the real reason. But do not accept him when he does pluck up the courage to ask you."

"I shall do as I choose, and you have no right to interfere! I am not Haymarket-ware for men to fight over!" Mary said furiously. "We are discussing Matthew's marriage, not mine!"

"Oh, but his marriage does not interest me nearly so much as yours, or mine," he replied blandly.

"Yours may interest you, but mine can be of no concern to you," she snapped, and again he chuckled.

"Well, then let us discuss Matthew's. Where are the culprits? Not fleeing for the border, I trust?"

"Teresa has a sick headache and is prostrate, poor girl. It's no wonder after all the excitement yesterday! Matthew seldom rises so early."

"So Teresa is fighting shy of meeting me, is she?"

"She is ill! I have seen her," Mary protested, annoyed at his insinuation and lack of feeling.

"Oh, yes, she is very convincing, I grant you. You have not had the advantage that I have of seeing these headaches develop whenever there is something distasteful to be done. She would recover in a miraculous fashion if you informed her that I had departed and there was to be an expedition to some milliner's shop."

"I am not surprised that Teresa is terrified of you," Mary commented acidly, having recovered her composure.

"So Teresa has favored you with her version of my character? I do hope I am never dependent on her veracity in a court of law! I would rate my chances low indeed! The fact remains that I am her legal guardian and that I will not permit her to make a fool of herself, which she would be doing by marrying your brother."

"Matthew is good enough to marry anyone," his sister declared, and Sir Ingram looked at her in amusement.

"Possibly. That is not what concerns me. Teresa is not fit to marry a boy who could not control her. Come, Miss Wyndham, you must confess that you would not like to see him married to a flighty, high-spirited girl who lacks all common sense and would give him not a moment's peace?"

"If that is the way it would be, no," Mary admitted. "Yet they maintain that they love one another, and surely she would not wish to do anything that might distress him, then?"

"She may not wish to, but she is thoughtless, vain, and selfish, having from her earliest years been permitted to do as she wished. When I took over her management two years since, she was almost past redemption."

"Maybe a husband who loves her would have more success!"

"Agreed, but not if he were himself dazzled by her and unwilling to bear with her tantrums. Besides, an elopement and the hasty marriage they planned would not look well. I propose sending both Teresa and her mother, who is equally bird-witted and lacking in sense, to my father's Aunt Hermione, who lives in Cheltenham. Removed from the temptations of London and guarded by our aunt, she may come to thank me in the end."

"I doubt it. I admit the elopement was not well done, but they were desperate and very much in love. What do you expect them to do?"

"Love is not the only consideration. And as Teresa has declared her undying love for at least a dozen men, you will see why I do not regard that particularly. Fortunately her father knew of this tendency, young as she was, and his will gives me the power to cut off her allowance until she is five-and-twenty if she marries against my will. I do not intend to allow her to marry a man who cannot support her and thinks to sponge on her fortune."

"You must have had undue influence over your uncle! It's a monstrous provision that makes it almost impossible for the girl to make her own choice, for it is clear you would not approve of anyone other than yourself!"

"So that part of her imagination is working again, is it?" was all he commented. "Teresa first imagined herself in love with one of my footmen, and then it was the painting master at her school. At least while she has been in society the social standing of her lovers has risen, but her constancy has if anything fallen. I would demand proof of a longer-standing attachment than the three weeks or so she has known your brother before consenting to a match."

"Then you do not forbid them to meet?" Mary said swiftly, recognizing that Teresa could not refuse to do as he wished and hoping to gain some comfort for the pair.

"Unless I kept her a prisoner, how could I prevent it?" he asked calmly. "I am no dragon, however she regards me. I put far greater dependence on her own volatility than on repressive measures. Besides, if I forbade them to meet, their elopement would become known, and I cannot wish for that to happen. Will you aid me in my deception?" he asked, leaning closer towards her and laughing down at her.

"I must, and I am grateful for Matthew's sake that you do not forbid them to meet."

"They must not meet alone, though, but in Cheltenham Teresa will be strictly chaperoned. I shall give it out that she is exhausted from all her racketing about and has gone to the country. Thank you for your hospitality, but I will now remove her to the inn and wait there for a message to be taken to Cheltenham, and also send for her mama to join us."

"Allow her to stay here, if you please. Since Papa seems to have known your father, it will be reasonable that she stays with me for a few days."

He looked at her with raised eyebrows. "It would be very kind of you. Can you offer her the chaperonage I insist upon when I am not able to undertake that duty?"

Mary grimaced at the idea of being regarded as a chaperone, but nodded.

"Naturally, or I would not have offered."

Sir Ingram laughed. "Then it is agreed, and I am most grateful to you. All that remains is to inform them."

He rose and extended his hand to help Mary to her feet, and she had just taken it when Caroline, her children with her, appeared.

"Mary, forgive me for interrupting. Susan said that you were out here, but not that you had a visitor!"

"Oh, I don't think she knew," Mary said, withdrawing her hand from Sir Ingram's in some confusion. "This is Sir Ingram Leigh, and his cousin is staying with us for a few days. Matthew has also come down from London. Sir Ingram's father knew Papa at Oxford. Sir Ingram, my dear friend, Caroline Grafton."

They uttered polite greetings, and Caroline, noting Mary's heightened color and making a swift but approving survey of Sir Ingram, smiled to herself.

"If you are staying here for a while, you must all come to the party my husband and I are giving tomorrow. We are not entirely dull in the country, you know."

"I would be delighted," Sir Ingram replied, "and I will accept on my cousin's behalf too. Teresa will no doubt have recovered from her headache by then," he added, with a laughing glance at Mary.

"Does she suffer from headaches? I do commiserate," Caroline replied feelingly, for she had often had severe ones herself recently. "But you will all come, which is delightful. Mary, I really came to deliver a message. I was walking with the children through the village, and Geoffrey Knowle asked me to inform you that he had been called out to a sick parishioner and so would be unable to call this morning."

Mary could not forebear glancing at Sir Ingram, but he was occupied in shaking out the folds of his coat and putting it on. As she turned back to reply to Caroline, however, his voice, so low that only she could hear it, came from behind her.

"Morning is not the most romantic time for a declaration, I agree."

When Caroline left to continue her walk, Sir Ingram departed to write his letters, saying that if it was convenient he would call later in the afternoon to speak with Teresa. Going back into the house, Mary found that Matthew had descended to the dining room and was gloomily partaking of a hearty meal. He looked up at her with a shamefaced grin and invited her to scold him for a silly gudgeon.

She laughed. In this mood he was irresistible, and though she chided him for being so thoughtless, she also comforted him with the news that Sir Ingram would not prohibit further meetings with Teresa, and had in fact agreed to her remaining under Mary's care until arrangements for taking her to Cheltenham could be made.

"How can I follow her there?" he demanded. "I have no money for at least a couple of weeks, until quarter day, and I know no one to give me credit in the town."

"Surely a mere two weeks, less for the time she spends here, will not matter unduly," she protested, but he shook his head.

"She is so lovely, there will be hordes of other men wanting to pay her attentions."

"Well, if you think her so fickle that she would desert you so easily, she is not fit to be your wife," said Mary in exasperation.

"She is young and used to being told what to do. Sir Ingram had permitted her so little freedom," he excused her, and Mary, deploring his infatuation, left him to go and see how Teresa was.

Smiling bravely at Mary, she appeared to receive Sir Ingram's edict that she was to go to Cheltenham within a few days with resignation.

"I might have known that Matthew and I could not have won," she murmured. "Now he will do his utmost to part us. Thank you for all you have done, Mary. I shall always be grateful, even if I never see you again. I begin to realize that I must not hope to escape him!"

"He will allow Matthew to see you," Mary said bracingly. "You have no cause for despair yet!"

Sadly Teresa shook her head. "That is what he tells you, but once he has me in his power again it will be different. And Aunt Hermione is a *gorgon*, truly she is! Her house is full of abominable lap dogs, and I have to take them for walks. It is almost the only freedom I get when I am forced to stay with her."

"Your mama will be there too, so no doubt she will be able to take you out."

The prospect did not seem to appeal to Teresa, for she muttered darkly that her mama would be too taken up with her precious Rodney to care what happened to her.

The rest of the day passed quietly. Sir Ingram called and was closeted with Teresa for twenty minutes, but Mary did not discover what had been said. Invited to remain for dinner, Sir Ingram excused himself, saying that he had discovered that a friend of his lived nearby and he intended to visit him. Teresa stayed in her room, and so for the first time the Wyndhams were alone and Matthew was able to explain to his father the reason for his and Teresa's unheralded appearance.

Beyond a slight admonishment about the folly of running away to marry, Mr. Wyndham did not seem unduly concerned. When Matthew lamented the fact that his impecuniary state would prevent his traveling to Cheltenham, Mr. Wyndham offered to advance him the quarter's allowance at once, saying that Matthew could repay him when the money due to him in a short time was available. With the prospect of being thus equipped to follow his beloved, Matthew's spirits revived astonishingly quickly, and since Teresa was not there, he decided to pay a visit to one of his old cronies in the village.

Left to herself, Mary's thoughts reverted to the conversation that morning with Sir Ingram. Matthew's affairs had been settled as satisfactorily as could have been expected, and he might still win his Teresa, though she was beginning to wonder whether that would be for his ultimate happiness. Sir Ingram might be right in saying that Teresa needed a strong man to control her. But it ought not to be Sir Ingram himself, Mary decided. That would be even less certain to result in happiness for either of them.

She recalled Sir Ingram's remarks about Mr. Knowle and realized that she had not given him another thought during the day. It was, she hoped, too late for him to call that evening, and so she would have a further respite before she had to give him an answer. She had no notion of what that answer would be. He could offer her a comfortable life, much the same as she had been living for the past few years, caring for a household. When he obtained his own parish there would be much for her to do. Could that satisfy her? Did she have any feelings towards him that might be deeper than mere friendship? she asked herself. He had indicated that he had a warm regard for her, but he had given no sign that those feelings went further than that. She could not imagine herself loving and being loved by Mr. Knowle as Caroline loved and was loved by Arthur. Would such love develop? There was nothing about Mr. Knowle to disgust her. Indeed he was a most handsome man, with polished manners, and came of an excellent family. With his connections he would find easy preferment, and might finish as a bishop. He would be kind always, considerate and generous, and would be a husband many girls would be envious of. Why did Caroline urge her not to accept? Did she place too high an emphasis on romantic love, having known it herself? And why, Mary thought with sudden indignation, had Sir Ingram interfered when it was certainly none of his affair?

Unable to solve these puzzles, Mary went to bed, but morning brought no enlightenment, and she spent the day in a fret of apprehension that Mr. Knowle would appear. However, dinnertime came and there had been no visit from him, and after the meal Mary went to fetch her shawl in readiness to walk to the manor.

Sir Ingram had not appeared at all that day, and Mary felt an irrational disappointment, but Teresa seemed not to care, saying that it was just like him to be unpredictable. They set off to walk the short distance between the two houses, and had almost reached the front door when a smart chaise drew up beside them and Sir Ingram leapt down to greet them.

"Well met, Miss Wyndham. Are you fully recovered, Teresa? Servant, Wyndham. I discovered that my friends, Paul and Belinda Ward, were coming to this party, and so I remained with them."

Paul and Belinda, children of a neighboring landowner, were old acquaintances, and Mary turned to greet them as they followed Sir Ingram out of the chaise. Then they all entered the house to be met by Caroline and her husband and found that there were already a dozen or so people there. Mr. Knowle detached himself from a group and came across to Mary, nodding coldly to Sir Ingram and the others before drawing her away, saying that Mr. Johnson, the vicar, who was in another room, had a message to give her for her father.

"He will not be staying long, and so asked to see you as soon as you arrived," he explained.

Caroline had organized dancing in her largest parlor, and card tables were set up for those of her guests who did not care to dance. After chatting for a while with Mr. Johnson, Mary was whisked away to dance by Paul Ward, a man a few years her senior who had known her all her life.

"It was a surprise to see Ingram," he began. "First time, to my knowledge, that he's been in this part of the world. I believe his father knew yours?"

"Yes, at Oxford. Is he a great friend of yours?" she asked curiously.

"We belong to the same clubs," Paul replied, "but he's a bit older than I am and has his own set. Very popular with the men as well as the women," he added, laughing. "He's an excellent whip, and shoots even better. And though he looks slight, he can hold his own with anyone in the ring."

"A *non pareil,* in fact," Mary commented briefly, and turned the conversation onto other subjects.

As the dance ended she found Mr. Knowle waiting to claim her attention.

"Miss Wyndham, pray will you spare me a few minutes?"

Unable to refuse, Mary felt her heart sinking as she realized what was to come. Mr. Knowle led her to the room where refreshments were laid out, secured a glass of orgeat for her, and then, remarking self-consciously that it was an exceptionally clear night and there were many stars to be seen, suggested that they stepped outside for a breath of fresh air.

"I do not dance, so I hope you will not refuse me this," he went on. "Not that I disapprove of it, mind, if not indulged in to excess, and so long as these shocking new dances such as the waltz are not permitted, but I do not consider it wise for a parson to partake of such pleasure. It sets a bad example."

Mary made a noncommittal reply and permitted him to lead her onto the terrace that ran along the whole of this side of the house. There were already two other couples there, and Mary was certain that one was Teresa and Matthew, but in the half-light she could not see clearly, and Mr. Knowle drew her away to the other end of the terrace.

"I think you must know what I have to say to you," he began without preamble. "I have your father's blessing and permission to pay my addresses to you, and so I am not acting hastily, unduly swayed by the beauty of the night, as I understand many men are. Mary—I hope you will permit me to call you that—I have for long admired, nay, loved you, and found in you all the most estimable qualities to be desired in a wife. I am asking you to make me the happiest of men by consenting to marry me. I realize that at the moment, in my present humble position, I have little to offer you, and that has constrained me from approaching you earlier. Now, however, I am about to be given the living in a small village near Bristol, and I shall have a home fit to take you to as well as an income, added to my own small means, which will keep you in comfort. I can say, without undue pride, that I hope to advance further in my chosen profession, and I know that you will adorn whatever position you are called upon to fill beside me. Mary, I trust that your answer is favorable?"

Mary took a deep breath, then slowly shook her head.

"I am sorry, Mr. Knowle," she answered in a low voice. "I—I cannot contemplate leaving my father. He needs me, and I must remain with him. I am aware of the honor you do me, but it would not be possible."

"Your sentiments do you credit, my dear. I take it that you do not have a personal aversion to me? That you might consider my offer if circumstances permitted it?"

"I—I have not really thought about it," Mary replied, wishing that somehow the ground would open and deliver her from this embarrassing situation. She did not love Mr. Knowle, but she respected him. How could she indicate that, without giving him hope for the future? She had not fully made up her mind to reject him, but she did not wish to encourage him unless she could really offer hope that eventually she would accept him.

"Well, who knows what might make it possible?" he said cheerfully. "I have not yet seen my new parish, but I am told that the house is commodious. Possibly your father, if he realizes that your happiness depends on it, would consent to come and live with us, and then our problems would be solved. You give me hope, my dear, and I am content for the moment. I shall be removing to Bristol in a month or so, and trust that we can come to a decision before then."

Without giving her time to reply, he turned to walk back into the house, and Mary, uncertain what she could have said, thankfully remained silent. When they entered the room, however, she found Sir Ingram with a small group of people seated there partaking of refreshment. He cast them a swift look and smiled mockingly at Mary before rising in a leisurely fashion to invite them both to join the group.

After a few minutes, while Mr. Knowle made stilted conversation and Mary remained silent, the strains of a waltz tune came from the parlor.

"May I dance with you, Miss Wyndham?" Sir Ingram asked, and Mary, unable to resist a somewhat guilty glance at Mr. Knowle, who had pursed his lips slightly, nodded assent and went off with him.

"He does not look the successful lover," Sir Ingram whispered in her ear as they circled the room. "I cannot believe that he did not take advantage of the starlight to make his offer?"

Mary frowned at him.

"You are impertinent, sir," she said quietly. "The fact that you have power over Teresa does not give you the right to dictate to me!"

"I would not dream of it," he murmured softly. "I can only give you advice, and that is not to marry the curate! If you want a better match, from the worldly point of view, there are many men who would be willing and able to give you all you wanted: but even more important is the fact that within a month he would drive you to despair. Can you contemplate forty years of his platitudes for breakfast?"

Despite herself Mary giggled at the thought, then remorsefully tried to excuse Mr. Knowle.

"He is stiff and shy with strangers, Sir Ingram. You judge him on too short an acquaintance. And I beg that you will refrain from giving me advice I do not desire and can do without!"

"On your own head be it, then," he replied with a laugh, and to her relief changed the subject, asking whether Teresa had said anything about her plans for the parrot. "I cannot see my aunt's dogs accepting such an addition to the *ménage* with complaisance, and had rather hoped that Teresa would be willing to send the creature back to town."

"I do not think that likely," Mary replied with a laugh. "She was maintaining today that he would be her only comfort while she was, as she put it, exiled from all her friends."

"Then I can only hope Aunt Hermione does not teach it even worse language than it possesses at present. Oh yes," he said in response to Mary's look of surprise, "the old lady was brought up in a far less squeamish age than our own, and her language can be exceedingly colorful when she is roused to anger."

"Then I am surprised that you can entrust Teresa to her," Mary commented.

He laughed. "When you meet Aunt Hermione and Teresa's mama, you will appreciate my problems," he told her.

There was no time for Mary to ask how in the world he expected her to meet either of them unless Matthew were permitted to marry Teresa, for the waltz ended, he led her off the floor, and the opportunity for private conversation was finished.

4

Within a few days the arrangements had been made, and Sir Ingram, who had accepted the Wards' invitation to stay with them, rode over to warn Teresa to make ready to leave on the following day.

"We are meeting your mama at Reading, providing she does not keep us waiting. Aunt Hermione writes that she will be pleased to have company for a few weeks."

"A few weeks! That is like to mean months," Teresa responded gloomily. "When will you allow me to return to London?"

"That depends on your behavior, in part," was all the satisfaction she received.

When he had departed, Teresa went reluctantly to her room to pack her belongings, and Matthew began to make his own plans for journeying to Cheltenham. Mary realized what he was about and sought for him, finding him in the stables.

"You cannot go with them," she said firmly.

"Why not? She is still terrified of him. Although he has behaved discreetly while he has been here and she has been under my protection, I cannot expect him not to ill-treat her once she is in his power!"

"You are being melodramatic!" Mary declared. "He will not harm her."

"He has previously beaten her, and she believes he has attempted to kill her," Matthew insisted. "Oh, I can see that he has bamboozled you with his surface charm! All women are alike and fall under his spell!"

"Excepting Teresa!" Mary rejoined sharply. "Truly, Matt, it would be more discreet for you to follow in a few days. Teresa will be with her mama in a few hours—"

"That is what *he* said!" Matthew interrupted.

"Oh, you are totally unreasonable! You behave like a dog protecting a bone rather than a adult contemplating marriage! Sir Ingram can prevent your ever marrying Teresa, or for many years, at least, but he has not said that he will. If you can behave sensibly now and show that you are capable of retaining Teresa's affections, he might relent, but if you annoy him he is less likely to. Is he proposing to remain in Cheltenham himself?"

"Is it likely?" Matthew asked scornfully, but Mary could see that her words had had some effect. She said no more, and merely nodded when that evening Matthew somewhat shamefacedly told her that he had decided to travel to Cheltenham two days later than Teresa.

On the following morning Teresa bade a cheerful farewell to Mary when Sir Ingram's chaise appeared. Freeing herself from the clinging embrace, Mary hurried from the room, leaving the lovers alone for the last few minutes. She intercepted Sir Ingram in the hall and detained him with what she realized were inane remarks. He eyed her with amusement and allowed her to ramble on until she could think of no more to say.

"Now that we have discussed the weather and the state of the roads—both, incidentally, unchanged for the past week—and the health of all our mutual acquaintances, do you think my cousin and your brother have had sufficient time for their farewell scene?" he inquired politely.

Mary laughed, tried to disguise it as a cough, and cast him a look of reproach.

"It is only kind," she managed.

"I have no intention of dragging her away by her hair, but since they will have ample opportunity of meeting in a few days' time, it might be kinder to cut short this painful moment."

"They will not be able to meet alone," Mary pointed out. "You have decreed that."

"But it is possible to be alone in a crowd, when waltzing, for example," he said softly, and Mary was furious to feel herself blushing.

Turning away abruptly, she led the way into the parlor, and soon Teresa was driven away, her parrot raucously protesting at this upheaval with a spate of words that Mary had not previously been privileged to hear from it.

For that day and the next Matthew miserably frittered away the time, favoring Mary with a monotonous catalogue of Sir Ingram's faults and Teresa's perfections, so that when early on the following morning he rode away, she was thankful to see him go and be able to return to the calm routine that had been so rudely shattered.

A week later, having received no word from Matthew in the meantime, Mary walked to the manor to visit Caroline. It was a bright, sunny day, and she walked slowly, reveling in the gentle breezes, the fragrant scents of summer, the sounds of insects and the twittering of the birds, and the distant cries from the farm workers bringing in the hay. Yet despite the perfection of the day, she felt dejected, a rare state for the normally contented Mary.

Caroline was not in the garden and Mary went

to seek her in the house, to be met by a worried-looking Arthur descending the stairs.

"Mary, Caroline sends her apologies, but she has a severe headache and is resting."

Mary looked at him anxiously. "Another headache?" she asked, for Caroline had been suffering from incapacitating headaches for some months. "I thought they usually came at night."

"They have done until this week, and were not very frequent, but she has had two in the last four days and both have lasted all day," Arthur said distractedly. "I don't think you ought to see her—she is best kept completely quiet."

"Of course, but is there anything I can do? What of the children? Can I take them for a walk? I don't suppose Betsy has time."

"Would you? They miss not going if Caroline for some reason cannot take them," he replied, and it was soon arranged.

They walked through the small park that surrounded the manor, and then across some hay fields, collecting bunches of wild flowers. When Mary decided that they had gone far enough, she turned into the woods that separated the farmland from the main road into the village and they wandered along beneath the trees, thankful for the shade, until they reached the edge of the woods and clambered over the stile into the road.

"Keep into the bank," Mary called, hearing the sound of a horse approaching, and the children obeyed her, turning and waiting for her to reach them. She smiled approvingly at them and gave them her hands, just as the horseman drew level and a well-remembered voice addressed her.

"A charming picture, Miss Wyndham," she heard, and swung round to look up into the laughing eyes of Sir Ingram Leigh.

"What are you doing here?" she asked, astonished. "I thought you would have gone back to London."

"Then you have been thinking of me?" he asked, and she frowned in annoyance.

"I cannot help wondering about Teresa," she retorted.

"Oh, what a set-down, when I had assumed it was myself you were concerned with. Rest content, she arrived safely and is chained hand and foot in an underground dungeon, fed on bread and water and regularly thrashed twice a day, three times if she complains of ill treatment!"

"Ooh!" came in awed accents from Peter, fascinated by this strange man.

"He is bamming you," Mary said crossly. "I pray you will not frighten the children, Sir Ingram!"

"They are too big to be afraid. Would you like to ride on my horse?"

Both Peter and Jane clamored for this treat, and Sir Ingram swung himself out of the saddle and lifted them both up, adjuring Peter to hold onto his sister. Then, looping the reins over his arm, he walked along beside Mary.

"She is sulking, as is my dear Aunt Cecy, but they will both soon find consolation," he told her, and she did not dare to ask whether this referred to Matthew or whether Sir Ingram had seen him before leaving Cheltenham.

"It was kind of you to ride over this way and tell me," she said stiffly, at which he laughed.

"Oh, I have not the slightest interest in them, as long as they cause me no trouble," he responded lightly. "I came back to stay with the Wards, since they very kindly pressed me to extend my visit. I was not acquainted with this part of the country previously, and find it has many attractions. You have lived here all your life, I understand?"

He maintained an easy flow of conversation and Mary relaxed, responding to his remarks and scarcely aware of her surroundings until they reached the gates of the manor. Then he halted and smiled down at her.

"I must leave you here, Miss Wyndham. May I call and talk again with your father one day?"

"I am sure he would welcome it," she replied, and he smiled again, then turned to lift down the excited children.

He mounted, and with a wave had turned and departed the way they had come. Mary walked once more along the manor drive, but this time, although she did not think of it, her unaccountable dejection had disappeared.

On the following day Caroline was completely better, and she and Mary went for a ride, as they often did. They had just enjoyed a gallop over a stretch of open country and reined in when a hail came from another group of riders who had just appeared from a patch of woodland. It was Paul and Belinda Ward, with Sir Ingram, and they rode over and exchanged greetings.

"We were coming to bring an invitation for you," Belinda said merrily. She was several years younger than Mary, and had only this year emerged from the schoolroom, so that neither Mary nor Caroline knew her as well as they did her brother. Now Mary looked at her with renewed interest. She was small, with a heart-shaped face, honey-gold curls, and laughing blue eyes. The horse she rode was a restive animal and pranced about as they talked, but she sat him with superb ease, obviously totally in control.

"My mother asks you to dine tomorrow evening," Paul explained. "Just a small party. Can you come?"

"We would love to," Caroline replied. "Mary?"

"Yes, and thank you."

"Then we will bring Mary with us," Caroline arranged briskly.

After a few more remarks they parted, and Caroline was unusually silent on the way home.

Mary was afraid that the ride had tired her and suggested that she should go straight home instead of remaining for the rest of the day as they had planned, so that Caroline could rest.

"Oh, do not be concerned. I am completely better," Caroline protested. "I was thinking, that is all."

"But these headaches are getting worse, are they not?" Mary persisted anxiously.

"Yes, and I have had one or two severe ones lately," Caroline admitted. "They are abominable at the time, but there are no effects the next day. Belinda is pretty, is she not?" she asked abruptly.

"I have not seen her often recently—only at your party, in fact. She has certainly changed from the schoolgirl she was."

"Sir Ingram seemed impressed. He danced with her twice at the party."

"He is obviously susceptible to feminine charms," Mary replied tartly, and Caroline smiled to herself and changed the subject.

The following day they drove to Abbey Court, the home of the Ward family, to find a group of twenty or so assembled for the dinner party, mostly young people who were nearly all known to Mary. As she entered the parlor Mary glanced quickly round, and then hastily turned her head away as she saw Sir Ingram leaning over Belinda's chair. Furious with herself for being concerned with his actions, she contrived to avoid him until they went in to dinner, when she found herself seated beside him, with Belinda on his other side.

"You appear cross," he said softly to her as they sat down, and chuckled at her glance of annoyance. "It must be very provoking to have to be polite to me when you are longing to tell me what a monster you consider me. Teresa was voluble on the journey, and left me in no doubt as to what she had told you of her side of the story. How much did you believe?"

"I am sure she exaggerated somewhat," Mary replied as coolly as she could, and he laughed again and turned to reply to a remark of Belinda's.

Scrupulously polite, he divided his attention between the two girls, but Mary, while conversing with her other neighbor, could not fail to be aware of how well he seemed to be getting on with Belinda.

Other people noticed it too, and there were many whispers to that effect when, dinner over, Mrs. Ward arranged for dancing in one of her parlors and Sir Ingram led out Belinda for the first set.

"They say he has ten thousand a year or more," one of the girls said to Mary. "Belinda will do well for herself if she can capture him! I wonder where they met?"

"I understand he is Paul's friend," Mary replied as casually as she could contrive.

"He seems more interested in Belinda, at any

event," was the response to this, and Mary had to admit to herself that it was true. Sir Ingram danced with several other girls but did not approach Mary, and later he danced again with Belinda, who looked radiantly beautiful in a cream and gold gown that suited her to perfection. Mary tried not to notice that after this dance Sir Ingram and Belinda disappeared for a while, and chided herself for being disturbed by it. On the drive home she was unusually silent, but Caroline forbore from comment, and only later, in the privacy of their bedroom, remarked to her husband that she thought Mary would do better for herself than Geoffrey Knowle after all.

"Oh? Whom do you mean? Paul Ward? He does seem attentive, I agree, but then he has known Mary all her life and never before shown any partiality for her."

"Not Paul, you simpleton," Caroline laughed. "I meant Sir Ingram."

"Sir Ingram Leigh?" Arthur said in amazement. "But he spent most of the time with Belinda!"

"Poof! That means nothing! It's either a blind or a ploy to make her jealous. I'm sure that as yet she has no idea."

"Well, neither had I," Arthur said with a laugh. "It's all in your imagination, my love."

"You haven't seen him looking at her when he thinks no one is watching," his spouse asserted with supreme confidence. "He certainly did not return to the Wards for the sake of Belinda's charms! You wait!"

Arthur began to think that his wife might be right when, on the following day, Sir Ingram appeared at the manor.

"Are you expecting Mary this afternoon, my love?" he asked, and received a blank look from his love.

"Oh, she often drops in, but there was nothing arranged," Caroline replied airily, and turned to her guest with a query about London.

After a time Arthur excused himself, saying that he needed to see to some matters on the farm, and Caroline offered to show Sir Ingram her gardens. They were in the rose garden when Mary appeared.

"Oh, I was not aware that you were here, Sir Ingram," she exclaimed.

"Or you would have gone away again, no doubt," he said softly as he took her hand and held it close for a moment. "I have been admiring Mrs. Grafton's roses," he went on in a louder voice, and turned back to Caroline to ask when she recommended pruning her bushes.

They went indoors and Caroline dispensed tea. She and Sir Ingram bore the brunt of the conversation, for Mary seemed abstracted. Caroline, more than ever convinced that her conjecture was correct, secretly rejoiced for her friend.

Eventually Mary said that she would return

home, and Sir Ingram instantly offered to escort her. While they were waiting for his horse to be brought round from the stables, Mr. Knowle was announced.

"Why, Mr. Knowle, it's an age since you have called on me," Caroline greeted him. "You shall stay and keep me company, for Mary and Sir Ingram are deserting me! How are the preparations for your removal coming along?"

Mr. Knowle did not appear to be anxious to stay, but politeness forced him to appear nonchalant as he watched the other two leave and Caroline bore him inexorably back into the drawing room.

"How long do you intend to remain with the Wards?" Mary asked, when they had covered half the distance towards her own home and she felt that the silence had become unbearable.

"I have not yet decided. It depends on many things, including the behavior of my dear cousin."

"Have you heard from Teresa? How is she?"

"I do not anticipate hearing from Teresa until she is frightened of the number of bills she has accumulated and needs me to pay them for her," he rejoined. "However, Aunt Hermione writes that she is well, and that your brother pays her assiduous attentions. I must admit that she has shown a preference for him for longer than I might have expected. For his sake I hope that it is not merely to demonstrate to me how badly I misjudge her!"

They had reached Mary's gate by now, and she suggested that he might care to visit her father.

"I thank you, but not today. I had not realized that it was so late, and have promised to return in time to escort Belinda to a party one of her friends is giving."

They parted, and Mary tried to distract herself from thoughts of Sir Ingram paying compliments to Belinda Ward by taking down from the shelves in the parlor those books which she and Matthew kept there and vigorously banging them to dislodge the dust that clung to them. Engrossed in her task, she looked up with suprise when Susan announced a visitor, for she had not heard the doorbell.

"Mr. Knowle, miss."

She rose to her feet, somewhat disheveled, and smiled nervously. He had not spoken to her alone since the night of the Graftons' party more than two weeks earlier, but as he was leaving Appleacre in less than a month, she knew that it could not be delayed much longer.

"Forgive me, I am not prepared for a visitor," she said, flustered.

"I do not mean to remain more than a few minutes, so pray do not disturb yourself. I came, my dear, to ask for an answer to the question I put to you some time ago. I think that I have given you ample time to consider it, and hope that your answer will be what I so earnestly desire to hear."

A confident smile on his face, he walked across the room and tried to take her hands in his, but she evaded him and slipped behind a chair.

"No. Mr. Knowle, I am aware that you will think me totally lacking in all consideration for you, but truly I cannot answer you! I esteem you, indeed I do, but I do not believe that I love you!"

He smiled, no whit put out. "That is not to be expected, my dear Mary. Indeed, I deplore those feelings which are romantically described as love, and indulged in by the unmarried. What can they know of true married love, sanctified by God? Their love, so-called, is but a fever of the blood and a sin to be condemned by all right-thinking persons. When we are married, love will come, have no fear."

Mary shook her head, wanting to protest that he was wrong but unable to find words to frame her thoughts. His smile grew a little less confident.

"I am leaving soon, Mary, and would like to begin preparing my new home to receive you. When will you marry me?"

"I have not said that I will!" she exclaimed. "Indeed, I am honored that you should ask me, should think me worthy of your lo— your regard, but I am not sure that I could live up to your expectations!"

"I will be the judge ot that, if only you will allow it. Now, may I tell your father that you have agreed to make me happy?"

"No. I beg you not to presume too early. I—I cannot give you an answer today!"

Angrily he stared at her. "I see how it is! You have had your head turned by that fashion plate from London! You imagine that he is paying court to you, and in your innocence do not realize that you are just one of the many that he sports with! Do not be a fool, Mary! Marry me, and do not hope for anything but dalliance from Sir Ingram Leigh!"

"He is *not* a fashion plate," she protested, as angry as he was. "And there has been no dalliance, as you so insultingly infer! He has no more thought to pay court to me than I have of receiving it! You had best go, Mr. Knowle, before we both say things that we would afterwards regret!"

She left the room precipitously and disregarded his attempt to call her back. Running up the stairs, she locked herself into her room and angrily flung herself down onto her bed. Hateful! Oh, how hateful to have him accuse her of dalliance—odious word—with Sir Ingram, who was more interested in Belinda Ward than he had ever been in her! The accusations did not even have the merit of being true, and she felt doubly insulted at the thought that she should be so misjudged. Furiously she fought back the tears and strove to calm herself, but she could not refrain from seeing in her mind pictures of Sir Ingram, and recalling his laughing eyes and attractive smile.

"Confound him *and* Mr. Knowle," she whispered to herself, when at last she had to prepare to join her father for dinner. Now she was at least certain that she could never accept Mr. Knowle's offer, since he could think such things of her, and she attempted to drag her mind away from these matters by taking an especial interest in her father's work.

The following week was a busy one. There seemed to have been a spate of dinner-party invitations in the district, mostly because of Sir Ingram's presence, Mary suspected, and she was forced to meet him at several houses and watch him apparently on excellent terms with Belinda, who seemed to be preening herself on her conquest. They also met a couple of times when out riding, and once again at the manor. The proposed visit to Mr. Wyndham had not yet taken place, and Mary did not know whether to be pleased that she did not have to entertain Sir Ingram, or sorry that he should appear to neglect her father.

Mr. Knowle kept discreetly in the background for a few days and then called again on Mary, pleading with her to forgive him, protesting that he had never meant to accuse her of unladylike conduct, and saying that he would wait a lifetime if only at the end of it Mary would make him happy.

Mary tried to make him understand that it would not do, and that she could never consider marriage with him. He chose to think that she was still offended and made it clear that he would continue to hope, and would go to his new parish in the confident expectation that she would eventually join him there.

These problems were then thrust into the background as Caroline, free for more than a week from her headaches, suddenly suffered three in as many days, and did not recover from this attack as swiftly as she had always done before.

One morning Mary was in the garden picking flowers when she saw Arthur approaching. Fearing that Caroline was again ill, she ran to meet him at the gate.

"How is she? Not ill again, I trust?"

"No, fortunately. But I wanted to see both you and your father."

Mary led him into the house and fetched her father from his study, and then Arthur explained the reason for his visit.

"The doctor has said that he thinks the headaches are from some nervous disorder, and he recommends a course of treatment at Bath. I cannot leave the farm for more than the few days necessary to escort Caroline to Bath and see her installed there, and I was hoping, Mary, that you would agree to go there with her. She will leave the children at home, naturally, for she could not be bothered with them if she were ill. But she will need company. There is a much older cousin of hers there, but they have a very small house and could not have her to stay. She must take rooms and would like you to go with her. You are her greatest friend. Will you do this for her?"

Mary shot an anxious look at her father. Much as she wanted to help Caroline, she had him to consider. He was smiling at her, however, and nodding.

"Yes, of course you must go, my dear. It will be a change for you, and you and Caroline will enjoy the company there. Do not worry over me. I have been thinking for some time that I would like to pay a visit to Oxford and see my old friend Anthony Drake. I did not wish to leave you, however. This solves the problem for us both."

Mary laughed in relief. "Then tell Caroline that of course I will be delighted," she told Arthur. "When does she intend to start?"

"In two days, if that is not too soon for you. We shall make the journey by easy stages, for fear that the driving affects her. Can you be ready? Of course we will delay it if you wish."

Mary assured him that she could be ready, and he departed, satisfied, while she began to sort through her wardrobe, enlisting Susan's help with her packing, and trying to organize at the same time her father's plans for his journey, which he proposed to start on the day after she left.

On her last evening Mr. Wyndham called her into the study, and, carefully unlocking the box in which he kept a store of coins, he handed her some bills and a *rouleau* of gold coins.

"I have not done all I could to introduce you to society, my dear," he said slowly. "I have been selfish, and for years mourned your mother too deeply to take any thought of pleasure. Then I became set in my ways. Arthur and Caroline will pay your main expenses, naturally, as you are their guest, but you will need money to buy some fashionable clothes. Take this, and when you need more write to me at Oxford. Yes, I insist. I can afford it, for I have not spent all my income these last years. Enjoy yourself, my child."

Touched, Mary kissed him, and left on the following morning in high spirits, conscious of a lightening of her heart as she left all her problems behind.

5

They made the journey in easy stages and Caroline suffered no recurrence of her headaches. Mary's first sight of Bath as they descended into the valley made her exclaim with pleasure.

"What a delightful setting! I never realized that it was like this!"

They stayed for two days at an inn while Mr. Grafton was busy inspecting lodgings. He discovered suitable ones in Queen Square and on the following morning took Caroline to see them. She was content with the view over the square and also the fact that it was close to the Pump Room, the baths, and the Assembly Rooms. Her only regret was that as soon as they were settled in Arthur must return to Appleacre.

"Let us hope that you will soon be well, my love, and then we need not be parted again," he comforted her. "I will make every effort to come and see you for a few days whenever I can spare the time from the farm."

On the next day, having seen them installed, he departed, and in order to take Caroline's mind off his going, Mary suggested that they begin to explore the town. They found much to please them, especially in the shops in Milsom Street, and Mary made several purchases in order to refurbish her wardrobe. When they returned to their lodgings they dined early and spent a peaceful evening sewing new braid and ribbons to their gowns.

Caroline was to begin treatment on the following morning, and after walking with her to the baths, Mary decided that she intended to do some more shopping. They had brought Susan with them to act as maid to them both, since she would have had nothing to do at home and Caroline's maid had been left behind to help take care of the children. She and Mary spent the next hour selecting muslins and silks which were to be made into gowns. Mary sent Susan home with the parcels at length, and strolled towards the Pump Room, where she had arranged to meet Caroline.

Entering this magnificent room, she looked

about her with some awe. Her experiences of public buildings was limited to the few assembly rooms near her home, and these in no way bore comparison with the room she now admired. Lofty and spacious, it was elegantly decorated and furnished, and the old woman handing the glasses of medicinal water to the visitors did so with the gracious air of a duchess condescending to serve wine to her guests.

As well as the room itself, the throng of visitors merited attention. There were many elderly ladies, some of them dressed in styles which would have adorned girls forty years younger, but which did worse than nothing to them, and some dressed in the outlandish fashions of their own girlhood which they had refused to abandon. Mary found it hard to decide which looked the more ridiculous.

Although most of the inhabitants of the Pump Room at this hour were women, there were a few men, and Mary's eye was immediately drawn to an "exquisite," posturing on heels too high for him. His coat was padded so that his shoulders appeared twice as broad as his waist, which was exaggeratedly pinched in. His coat was of a sickly-hued pink and his pantaloons of a darker shade, matched by the leather boots with high heels. As he twirled about to address another of the group surrounding him, she saw that his shirt fronts were too high to permit his head alone to turn, and then her glance fell to his hands, flashing fire from the several rings he wore and holding an elegant short cane with which he was gesticulating in order to emphasize a point.

"Isn't he a fright?" Caroline asked, coming up to her and seeing what held her attention.

Mary laughed. "Are there many like him? If so, I shall be hard put to it not to laugh in their faces!"

"He's the best I've seen so far," she was informed. "But come across and meet my aunt and cousin. They live in Bath, and I had intended to call on them this afternoon, but they are here now."

Mary was introduced to a friendly, middle-aged woman, Mrs. Wright, and her son Jonathan, who was about her own age, and then to several people sitting with them.

"Caroline, my love, it is so nice to see you, though I do hope your illness is soon cured. It is a pity that I could not have offered you a room, but as you know, we have very small lodgings. I must introduce you to my friends, though, and you will not lack for company while you are here."

She did as she had promised, and soon Mary and Caroline were swept into a whirl of parties. On the first occasion that they attended a ball at the Assembly Rooms, they saw again the exquisite who had been such a source of amusement in the Pump Room. He did not appear to dance—

probably because he was corseted so tightly that he could not bend, Caroline speculated laughingly—neither did he spend his time playing cards. Instead he paraded round the room, graciously acknowledging acquaintances, and remaining to talk with them for a while.

It was when Caroline was going with her partner to the tea room and had to pass behind him that the accident occurred. Just as Caroline was next to him he stepped backwards with an extravagant gesture, and the silly little heel of his shoe caught in the hem of Caroline's gown and tore it. She uttered a cry of dismay, and the dandy, who had heard the sound of the rending material, swung round to extricate himself from the disaster, full of profuse apologies for his carelessness.

"Madam! It is that I am so clumsy! A million apologies! I pray you accept the most humble abasement of your servant! What in the name of the goddess of beauty can I do to repair the damage I have wrought? But tell me, and I will fly to the moon and back for you!"

Torn between laughter and annoyance, Caroline retorted that it would be more appropriate if he had needle and thread, and to her astonishment he delved into the pocket of his coat and produced these items.

"Oh, that I should not have thought of it for myself. I am *imbecile,* truly! But I beg that you will accept these from me as a small gift, slight recompense for having discommoded you. I am unlikely to need them for myself, in any event, this evening, and I can instruct my good Yves to replace them before I next venture into the world!"

Caroline, choking with laughter, escaped, and regaled Mary with her imitation of this ridiculous encounter when they returned to their lodgings.

"He is an utter fool, Mary, and his fake French accent sends me into whoops! I wonder who on earth he can be?"

They were to find out the following morning, for when, as was their custom, they met in the Pump Room, the dandy was there, and the moment he espied Caroline he made a beeline for her, drawing considerable attention to them both as he forged his way through the strollers and came to rest before her.

"Madam, again I crave your gracious forgiveness for my incredible stupidity last night. I do hope that your gown—so delightful a gown, truly—is not ruined utterly beyond repair?"

"Oh, no, I was able to stitch it," Caroline responded coolly, not anxious to prolong the meeting. He had other ideas, however:

"I believe I have seen you with my friend, Mrs. Wright. Am I correct? Then pray allow me to introduce myself. As an old friend of your friend you will not, I feel sure, take it amiss of me to do so. Madam, your humble servant, Rodney Morris!" he concluded with a flourish.

Mary's eyes widened in astonishment. That was the name Matthew had mentioned as a friend of Teresa's mama. Without waiting for Caroline to introduce her, she spoke.

"You must know Mrs. Standish, I believe?"

"Indeed I do have that honor."

"Is she still at Cheltenham, do you know? And her daughter?"

He shook his head. "No, they arrive in Bath later this very day. But how is it that you know so much, Miss—er—?"

"I beg your pardon. I am Mary Wyndham. My friend, Mrs. Grafton," Mary hastily introduced them. "I understand that they stayed with an aunt?"

"Indeed, you are correctly informed, Miss Wyndham. I begin to discern a way out of this so strange a maze. You are, I take it, a connection of Mr. Matthew Wyndham?"

"His sister, yes, but how is it that they come to Bath?"

"They will be with us all soon if nothing goes amiss on the journey. It is simple enough, for the good lady, Mrs. Leigh, decided that the treatment at Cheltenham was not for her as successful as she expected, and she determined on removing herself and her guests to Bath. I volunteered to come in advance and secure a house for them, and I am happy to say that I have succeeded in my little mission. Your brother, he escorts the ladies, and I have no doubt that you will soon be reunited with him."

"I see," Mary said slowly, wondering whether this incursion into fashionable Bath society was quite what Sir Ingram had envisaged when he had banished Teresa to stay with her aunt.

"I have no doubt that we shall meet with them soon," Caroline said briskly. "And now, Mr. Morris, if you will excuse us, I have some purchases to make."

Eventually they escaped from his bows and apologies and were able to discuss this new development.

"You might have an ally in Mrs. Standish," Caroline suggested. "That is, if you wish to encourage the match."

"I am not at all sure that I do," Mary confessed. "Teresa was amiable enough, and she appeared to have been shockingly oppressed by Sir Ingram, but she is the first girl Matthew has fallen in love with, and it did happen decidedly quickly. I had far rather they waited a few months to be sure that it is a lasting attachment."

"Do you believe all the things she told you?"

"She probably exaggerated her tales of ill treatment, and as for the attempts on her life—they *could* have been accidents—I cannot think she told deliberate lies, and if it were a tenth as bad as she claimed, it were bad enough. I wonder if her mother is really so incapable as Sir Ingram suggests?"

"If she in any way resembles Mr. Morris, yes! How any woman could bear to have so foppish a creature as a friend, I cannot tell!"

They were to meet Mrs. Standish the following day. Once more Mr. Morris approached them, but this time to beg them to allow him to introduce his dear friend to them.

"Mrs. Standish does so wish to thank you for protecting her ewe lamb from the ferocity of that abominable cousin of hers," he said as Mary and Caroline crossed the room to where Mrs. Standish sat awaiting them.

She was a faded blond, her hair dressed in childish ringlets, and her complexion owing a great deal to art. She extended a plump hand to Mary when they were introduced and beamed on her.

"My dear child's savior! How can I ever thank you for preserving her? My dear Miss Wyndham, you were heroic, indeed you were. Heaven only knows what would have happened to my baby if Ingram had caught up with her before she had reached the haven of your arms!"

"I cannot think that he would have harmed her, ma'am," Mary replied soothingly.

"Oh, you do not know him as I do. I am the most unfortunate of women, to have been left with him the arbiter of my fate. He is a monster, my dear, with no finer feelings! He has no appreciation of the trials of a widow; no care for my comfort; no notion of how a mother feels when her only child is tortured and threatened and she has no power to prevent it! And he would have me deliver my precious baby into his power to an even greater extent by permitting her to marry him! Rather would I cast myself from the dome of St. Paul's!"

"Where is Teresa, ma'am?" Mary asked faintly, as this spate of complaints came to an end. Mrs. Standish looked about her vaguely, as though suddenly recalled to her surroundings.

"Are they not here? Rodney, where is Teresa? Has the naughty one slipped away with Mr. Wyndham? Oh, well, girls will be girls! It is a fortunate chance that Aunt Hermione is not here this morning! But that puts me in mind of something. I am so glad to have seen you, Miss Wyndham, for when Mr. Morris informed us that you were in Bath, Aunt Hermione said that you were to be sure to come to her party tonight. Just a small affair, you know, for her acquaintances that are in Bath. Mrs. Grafton, you are to come too, of course. We have taken a house in Great Pulteney Street, and will be delighted to welcome you there. Oh, there is dear Sir Bernard! Rodney, pray desire Sir Bernard to step across and speak with me. Good-bye then, dear Miss

Wyndham, and Mrs. Grafton, until tonight!"

They edged away, speechless, avoiding one another's eyes, and did not dare to comment until they were safely outside the Pump Room.

"Oh, Mary, my sides are aching with trying not to laugh!" Caroline gasped. "She and that precious Mr. Morris are indeed well matched! How *could* Teresa have a mother like that?"

"She had little say in the matter," Mary laughingly pointed out. "Oh, yes, she is comical, but surely there must be something against Sir Ingram for her to be so vehement against him!"

"I have no doubt that she has imagined it all and has influenced Teresa against him!" Caroline declared roundly. "I wonder what Aunt Hermione is like? If she is anything like these two, I shall be hard put to it to behave in a seemly fashion!"

"None of them appear to be chaperoning Teresa properly," Mary said worriedly, but Caroline laughed at her.

"What nonsense! In Bath! It is the most sedate of places, my dear. What harm can there be if they do slip away for a quiet talk on occasion? No doubt they merely walk in the parks."

"Nonetheless it will cause comment, and I cannot feel it wise of Matthew to flout convention so. It will most likely offend Sir Ingram, on whose good offices he must depend if he is to gain permission to marry Teresa."

She found that she had even greater cause to

be concerned that evening, for Matthew, when he arrived at Mrs. Leigh's party soon after Mary and Caroline, immediately attached himself to Teresa and remained determinedly at her side. Mary had no opportunity to intervene, however, for Mrs. Standish swept down on her and carried her off to be introduced to Mrs. Leigh, who sat enthroned in the drawing room. Aunt Hermione looked magnificently autocratic, but Mary immediately warmed to her when, on being introduced by a dithering Mrs. Standish, Mrs. Leigh waved that lady firmly aside and patted the seat beside her invitingly.

"Do sit down, my dear. I have wanted to thank you for behaving so sensibly when little Teresa came to you. You would seem to have more wit in your little finger than the child's mother and that mincing nincompoop that trails after her, put together!"

Mary could not forbear laughing as she sat on the sofa, carefully avoiding the spreading skirts of stiff brocade that Mrs. Leigh, faithful to the fashions of her youth, still affected.

Mrs. Leigh nodded, the tall ostrich plumes in her hair waving vigorously.

"Yes, I can read between the lines from what Teresa told me. Your brother must have more hair than wit to have carried her off in that addlepated fashion! Not the best way to get Ingram to agree to a match, for he's a stickler for the proprieties! I've warned him what would come of it, but Teresa hasn't the spirit to rebel properly!"

She chuckled at Mary's astonished look and wagged a bony finger at her.

"You would scarce advocate rebellion, surely, ma'am?"

Mrs. Leigh grinned at her, her bright eyes gleaming with mischievous amusement.

"You young folk cannot seem to get it into your heads that my generation has not always been gouty and in need of taking the waters! We have lived too, in our day, and in my youth we had more daring than young people have today. You'll find it hard to credit, no doubt, but I assure you that Mr. Leigh and I managed our elopement a great deal better than this pair did! Oh yes," she went on, chuckling as she saw Mary's startled glance, "I eloped too, but I succeeded in getting married as well! Mr. Leigh was the younger brother of the Sir Ingram of the time, this one's grandfather, and his family disapproved of me because my father had made his money in India. Very high in the instep, they were! A connection with trade would sully their family name, they thought—though most of them have not since allowed that connection to deter them from sponging on me whenever it suited them! *That's* no dishonor! Not Ingram, for he's a good boy, and in any event has a fortune as big as mine, but all the rest of the brood! Tell your brother that if he behaves properly Ingram will be bound to come round. Even though Mr. Wyndham hasn't shown a deal of sense so far, I like him. He'll deal well with Teresa, for he's a good, straightforward lad, and she's not overburdened with sense anyway. She'd drive a more sensible man to distraction within a se'nnight!"

Mary was tempted to ask whether the old lady thought it possible that Sir Ingram wished to marry his cousin. He did not appear to need her fortune, and was undoubtedly a sensible man. Before she could frame these questions, however, Mrs. Leigh was dismissing her, saying that she wished to speak with one of her friends, and so Mary had to give up her seat to the next favored guest.

Thoughtfully, Mary moved away. She had taken an immediate liking to the forthright Mrs. Leigh, and was grateful for her muted praise of Matthew. However, was she chaperoning Teresa effectively? When she delegated that task to Mrs. Standish, as she had that morning, it did not appear that Sir Ingram's intentions were being adhered to. In addition to that, Mary was concerned that the history of Mrs. Leigh's youthful elopement would merely prove to be an added spur to Teresa. It would most decidedly not convey to her how reprehensible her own behavior was.

Caroline was occupied talking to some friends,

so Mary went to look for Matthew and Teresa. She rather doubted whether her remonstrances would be effective, but she felt bound to make an attempt to reason with the lovers. They were not in the drawing room, and she went downstairs to a parlor where some of the younger guests had gathered. There she discovered them, sitting together near a window at the far end of the room, and so absorbed in their low-voiced conversation that they paid no heed to the group gathered about the harpsichord, singing, nearer to the door.

They looked up as Mary spoke, and as she halted before them Matthew rose to his feet and offered her his chair. With an understanding smile she took it.

"I've been talking to your aunt, Teresa. She seems hopeful that Sir Ingram will relent in due course."

Teresa looked at her skeptically.

"She gave me a shocking scold earlier," she replied despondently. "Just because she had heard, from one of the inquisitive old pussies that came to visit her this afternoon, that Matthew and I had been walking in Spring Gardens without Mama."

"Well, it is not wise of you to attract gossip," Mary said calmly. "That is not the way to win Sir Ingram's approval."

"Confound Sir Ingram! He is opposing Teresa because of his own wicked designs!"

"Oh, come!" Mary laughed uncertainly. "I find it difficult to believe that."

"You do not know him!" Teresa declared. "He wants to marry me, or if he cannot gain control of my fortune in that way, he will murder me!"

"Do not be ridiculous!" Mary exclaimed. "You put me out of all patience with you when you make such wild accusations. All those so-called attempts on your life were but accidents!"

"I am enchanted to discover that you, at least, Miss Wyndham, do not condemn me for a black-hearted villain!" a deep, amused voice said, and they all turned in astonishment to find Sir Ingram standing beside Mary's chair, regarding them with a sardonic look.

Mary flushed and, as she encountered his disturbing glance, looked hastily away. Matthew seemed uncomfortable, but Teresa was the least perturbed of the three.

"What brings you here?" she demanded pettishly. "I thought I was free of you for a while!"

"A charming welcome from my so delightful cousin," he responded mockingly. "Are you not delighted to see me?"

"No, for you have doubtless come to spy on me!" she replied frankly, and he raised his eyebrows, grinning at her.

"You make the mistake, my dear, of considering your own affairs as absorbing to the rest of us as they are to you."

"If people are not concerned, why do they spend all their time tittle-tattling!" Teresa asked, annoyed.

"Do they, indeed? From that I infer that you have been giving cause for gossip," he rejoined.

Teresa flushed in annoyance. "Then why are you here?" she repeated.

"Oh, I have matters of my own to attend to," he replied, aggravatingly. "It seems fortunate, however, that I will also be able to undertake my share in the task of controlling you. Aunt Hermione is not so well as I had hoped, and needs more assistance than Miss Wyndham can provide."

"I am not responsible for Teresa now!" Mary interjected, annoyed.

"Oh? I had rather hoped that you might be persuaded to take an interest in her welfare," he replied smoothly, smiling down at her.

She could not interpret the expression in his eyes, but it discomposed her, and she looked hastily away.

"Do you mean to stay here?" Teresa persisted.

"No, my dear. You shall not be constrained to suffer my company at breakfast! I mean to take rooms."

"For how long?"

He shrugged. "Who can tell? Until my affairs here are concluded satisfactorily, no doubt."

Teresa glowered at him, and he laughed, then turned to Mary.

"Miss Wyndham, I have yet to pay my respects to my aunt, for she did not expect me this evening. Will you honor me when I return, and have supper with me?"

Mary scarcely had time to murmur a surprised acceptance before he had bowed himself away. Teresa broke into immediate complaints, interspersed with fruitless speculations as to what motive Sir Ingram could possibly have for coming to Bath other than to persecute her. Matthew did his best to soothe her, but she refused to be consoled, and Mary was relieved when, in a surprisingly short time, Sir Ingram reappeared to lead her away to the dining room where a buffet supper had been spread.

He chatted easily as he helped her to lobster patties and jellies, poured wine for her, and installed her at one of the small tables scattered about the room. The tumult of emotion, which she decided was due to surprise mingled with apprehension, subsided as he talked, commenting amusingly on the people at the party and asking who else she had met during her few days in Bath. She responded to his lead, and they were soon laughing as she told of their encounter with Mr. Morris at the Assembly Rooms.

"My uncle was not an especially sensible man," he remarked, "but Aunt Cecy was truly devoted to him. What she sees in this nincompoop is beyond me. You understand now why I have problems in insuring that Teresa is properly cared for!"

"She is young, and afraid of you, I think," Mary ventured.

"You evidently discredit her wilder charges as to my villainy?"

"She is too imaginative, seeing herself as the persecuted heroine of some romance. I doubt if she really believes them herself," Mary replied.

Before he could answer, Mrs. Standish joined them, and there was no further opportunity for private talk. Soon afterwards Mary and Caroline left the party, and Caroline, noting her friend's abstracted air, smiled to herself and confined her remarks to innocent chatter about the people she had met and her impressions of Mrs. Leigh.

Mary, having had time to consider this new development, decided that she was relieved at Sir Ingram's arrival, since he could undertake the task of chaperoning Teresa. The following morning, when she had been forced to listen to two elderly dowagers casting severe strictures on Teresa's behavior, she began to think that he had come just in time to preserve his cousin's reputation by exercising a control no one else seemed capable of.

She extricated herself from this conversation, and was crossing the Pump Room towards Mrs. Wright when she heard her name called. Turning, she found Paul Ward at her elbow.

"Miss Wyndham! How pleasant to meet you so soon!"

"Mr. Ward! I had no notion that you were in Bath!"

"No, we arrived yesterday. My parents decided to come here this year instead of Tunbridge Wells, and they have taken a house in the Royal Crescent. Belinda will be pleased to find some friends here."

"Is she here now?" Mary asked, her spirits unaccountably falling as she heard this.

"No, she has gone to Milsom Street, and will no doubt be there all morning! But here comes Mrs. Grafton."

Caroline was approaching, and expressed her surprise at the meeting. Promises were made that they would call on Mrs. Ward, and then Mary and Caroline left, planning to walk in the gardens beside the river.

They had barely turned towards the abbey, however, before Mary halted, clutching at Caroline's arm.

"What is it?" Caroline asked.

"Mr. Knowle. Over there, looking into that shop window. I do not believe he has seen us. Let us turn away. I cannot face a meeting with him at this moment! There are too many of our acquaintances suddenly appearing in Bath!"

It was too late. As she spoke, Mr. Knowle turned, saw them, and with a beaming smile crossed to greet them.

6

"*My dear Mrs. Grafton,* and Miss Wyndham! How opportune a meeting. I was proposing calling at your lodgings, although I had little expectation of finding you there at this hour. I trust that the treatment is effective, Mrs. Grafton, and that you are feeling more the thing?"

"Indeed yes, Mr. Knowle. I have not had a severe headache since I arrived. But what a surprise to see you here!"

"Not an unpleasant one, I hope. I am on my way to my new living and spent last night here, intending to see you today. Mr. Grafton entrusted me with messages and a letter."

"How kind of you to trouble with that," Caroline

said, taking the small packet he produced. "I hope it has not inconvenienced you at all?"

"Not in the least. Apart from the pleasure it gives me of seeing you both, I wished to halt for the last night within a short distance of my final destination, so that I can arrive there in good time. I must finish my journey tomorrow, and hoped, if you had no other engagements, that you would dine with me at my hotel tonight?"

As it happened they had no other engagement, and after a quick glance at Mary, Caroline accepted for them both. Mary had not yet spoken, apart from greeting Mr. Knowle, for she knew that he had sought them out in order to press for an answer to his proposal, and despite much thought she still could not make up her mind finally to accept him. Now she made an effort to behave normally and asked after some of the parishioners he had left.

When they seemed to have no more to say on that head, he suggested that if they had time he would enjoy seeing the abbey in their company, and so they retraced their steps past the Pump Room while Mr. Knowle told them that he had long wished to see the site of the church where King Edgar had been crowned so many hundreds of years ago, but that he had never before visited the city.

They admired the lovely carvings on the west front, and then entered the abbey to look at the interior, afterwards walking round to inspect some of the tablets erected to the memory of former illustrious inhabitants of the town. Mr. Knowle explained reluctantly that he had another message to take from Mr. Johnson to an old friend of his who lived in Henrietta Street.

"I wonder if you could give me directions?"

"We will walk with you as far as Pulteney Bridge," Caroline offered, "and then it is on the far side, off Laura Place."

They set him on his way and then returned to their lodgings to rest before the dinner hour.

"You did not object to my accepting his invitation?" Caroline asked anxiously. "I do not like the man, but felt that it would be churlish to refuse, as he is a stranger to the town."

"It was polite, but I beg of you, Caroline, do not make any excuse to leave us alone, for I know that he will want an answer and I have not yet decided what I can say to him!"

"If it takes you so long to make up your mind, then you cannot love him," Caroline declared. "You would not hesitate if you really loved him, so why not end his hopes and refuse him?"

"I did, when we were at home, but since he had accused me of dalliance with Sir Ingram, and I grew angry, he would not accept that as final, and I confess, when he came back and craved my pardon, I had not the heart to do other than say I would consider it. Caroline, it is not so simple! I do like him, as a friend, even though he appears stiff at times. He—he says that love would come, and many people do, I am aware, marry without such feelings in the beginning. If I were to marry him, my father could live with us and would have congenial company."

"You do not marry for the benefit of your father!" Caroline pointed out with some acerbity, and Mary reluctantly laughed.

"No, but he has always been a consideration. I could not leave him alone! And I have begun to think of what I will do when he is gone. We have so few relations, none that would be able to receive me into their homes, and I cannot envisage myself living with Matthew and Teresa, provided that he eventually married her!"

"Indeed not! Or with whomever he marries. But why should you regard Mr. Knowle as your only alternative? Jonathan has been attentive, and he is not the only man to have paid you compliments."

Mary shrugged. "Politenesses, all of them, and meaningless."

"Nonsense, child! You have lived so secluded a life that you have met few men of the world, and cannot know what your effect on them is! Added to that, you are reserved, and they find it difficult to get on easy terms with you. That is why I think you like Mr. Knowle, for you have known him for so long and he is so puffed up with his own consequence that he is not afraid of you!"

"Am I so awe-inspiring, then?"

"No, shy, merely. I am conscious that it is very impertinent of me to offer advice, but I love you and cannot bear to see you ruin your life. Do not accept Geoffrey Knowle, Mary! He is not the right man for you!"

"Who is?" Mary queried, amused and not at all offended by her friend's remarks.

"I think you know, except that you will not allow yourself to entertain the notion," Caroline said, and then quickly excused herself, saying that she wished to lie down for an hour, but in reality to give Mary an opportunity of considering her remarks.

Mr. Knowle put himself out to be entertaining, and had ordered an excellent meal of roast capons, a ragout, mutton cutlets, and a rabbit pie, with trout and side dishes of peas and salads. Fruit tarts, cheese, and a syllabub followed, and he had also obtained excellent wines from the hotel's cellar.

They ate in his private sitting room, and when the waiters had removed the covers he apologized that they had nowhere to withdraw.

"I am not one to wish to sit drinking after a meal, however," he laughed, and explained that he had ordered tea to be brought in half an hour.

"It has been very pleasant," Mary said, and he smiled at her fondly.

"I am hoping that I can persuade you both to drive over to see me in my new home before you leave Bath. It is less than a dozen miles, and if you drove over in the morning we could have an early dinner and you could return before dark. Perhaps Matthew would escort you. I had not realized that he was in Bath also."

"Have you seen him?" Mary asked in surprise.

"Yes, although he did not see me. I was returning from my visit to Mr. Johnson's friend, and when I entered Laura Place I saw him on the far side, talking with a young lady. I could not be sure, for she had a scarf about her head, but it looked remarkably like the young lady who stayed with you at Appleacre. Miss Standish, was it not?"

"Yes, she is in Bath," Mary admitted.

"Are you staying with her? I had not understood that you knew her so well."

"No, she is here with her mother and a great aunt, who is taking the waters."

"And Matthew? I assume he came to bear you company. I would have invited him this evening had I known earlier that he was here. Seeing him was such a surprise, but I did not care to intrude on them, and the notion did not occur to me until I had walked on over the bridge. Very slow of me, I fear!"

"Matthew lodges in Lansdown Road," Mary said evenly.

"Then he will no doubt accompany you. Let me see, next week might be rather too soon for my housekeeper, and I ought to spend the first few days getting to know my parish. Shall we make it the week after next, on the Thursday? Would that be convenient?"

Unable to think of an excuse for refusing the invitation, and uncertain of her reasons for resisting the idea, since it provided an opportunity of seeing this house which might soon be her home if she accepted Mr. Knowle, Mary agreed. It was settled that they would drive over on the day proposed.

"If Matthew has other plans, I am sure my cousin would be happy to escort us," Caroline added.

Soon afterwards the tea was brought in, and then, with good wishes expressed by all, Mr. Knowle conducted them down to the carriage Caroline had ordered to fetch them.

On the following morning Mary met Teresa in the Pump Room. She was looking decidedly put out, and Mary inquired what was amiss.

"It is most unfair that because Ingram has heard spiteful gossip he refuses to permit me to go on the expedition we had planned to Wookey Hole, and I had been so looking forward to it!"

"Wookey Hole? Is that not the ancient cave near to Wells? I would have thought it too far to drive there and back in one day."

"That is the difficulty. A party of us had arranged to go, and we were to remain the night in Wells, where there is an excellent inn, and ride back on the following day. Now Ingram says that there is no one to chaperone me, for Mama does not ride, you see. We will not be able to go—unless—I have it! Would you and Mrs. Grafton come with us? Mama thinks highly of you, and Mrs. Grafton is a respectable married lady, so that would satisfy the old cats of Bath! Even Ingram could not object if you were to join the party. Oh, Mary dear, please say that you will!"

Mary smiled at her, grateful that Teresa had refrained from saying that she, at her age, would make a suitable chaperone.

"It is a tempting plan," she said slowly. "I cannot speak for Caroline, and it would mean that she missed her treatment for two days. I do not know whether that would be wise."

"We can ask her when she comes. But do come across to Mama and put the idea to her."

Mary accompanied her to where Mrs. Standish and Mrs. Leigh sat, with Mr. Morris hovering about in the background, and Teresa excitedly explained her new plan. Mrs. Leigh smiled at Mary approvingly.

"Well, if Mrs. Grafton will go, I think Ingram can be content. Besides Teresa and Matthew there will be a family of two girls, friends of ours, their brother, and a cousin. They suggested that Teresa join them and she has given us no peace since!"

"It will be such an agreeable expedition," Teresa said persuasively.

"I cannot imagine why you should want to see inside dirty horrid dark caves," Mrs. Standish shuddered.

"We also propose to visit Wells Cathedral, and that will be most informative," Teresa remarked. "Mr. Morris has been telling me all about it."

"A very impressive example of cathedral architecture," Mr. Morris contributed.

"Mr. Morris has agreed to accompany the party," Mrs. Leigh told Mary, "but Ingram would not permit her to go without an older woman to chaperone her. With you and Mrs. Grafton there, he can be content. You both have a great deal of sense."

Caroline appeared at that moment and was instantly appealed to by Teresa. Seeing that Mary was willing to join the expedition, she made no objection, saying that she had been feeling so much better since being in Bath that to miss the treatment for just two days would not matter in the least. It was arranged that the rest of the party would call for Mary and Caroline early on the following morning, and then they parted, Teresa beaming happily at Mary as she bade her good-bye.

Somewhat to Mary's surprise, when they met the others it was to find the party enlarged by the inclusion of Sir Ingram himself and the Wards. Mary found herself watching Sir Ingram as he rode beside Belinda up into the hills surrounding the town, unsure of whether these additions to the party were an improvement or not. Certainly it would relieve her of most of the responsibility for Teresa, but she found his company disturbing, and Belinda's vivacity irritated her unduly.

Teresa, unlike the high-spirited Belinda, was sulking, apparently because of her cousin's presence, and responding shortly to Mr. Morris's valiant attempts to converse with her.

Mary had been surprised at Mr. Morris's unexpected ability as a horseman. He had appeared, exceedingly elegantly attired, mounted on a nervy chestnut which had sidled and fretted restlessly as they had negotiated the town. Mr. Morris had been unperturbed, paying the animal no more than the minimum of attention and yet controlling it where many other riders would have been defeated. Once out of the town, he had led them in an exhilarating gallop, and Mary had further admired his masterly control over the animal.

Matthew was carefully avoiding Teresa, and his prudence no doubt contributed to her peevishness. He came to ride beside Mary and Caroline, and Mary tried to distract his attention by commenting on the scenery and asking what he knew of the caves they planned to visit. He was exceedingly well informed.

"They have been worn hollow by the river that runs through them. Men are supposed to have lived in them many hundreds of years ago, and skeletons have been found, as well as pottery and tools and jewelry. There are huge stalagmites and stalactites, and one of them is called the Witch of Wookey."

"What a peculiar idea," Caroline commented.

"I suppose it is because long ago there was a witch who lived in the caves, and the local people had to ask the abbot of Glastonbury to aid them in getting rid of her. I do not think it is known what he did, but she apparently disappeared, and people may have thought that she had been turned into this stalagmite."

The party had set out very early, but it was well into the afternoon before they had covered the eighteen or so miles to the caves. Leaving their horses at an inn some way from the entrance, they walked upward through the valley, exclaiming at the magnificence of the tumbling river gushing along its rocky bed, with the overhanging trees crowded into the narrow defile.

The interior of the caves was quite as impressive as Mary had anticipated. They clambered down steep, uneven steps, through lofty chambers where the light from the lanterns their guides carried did not penetrate to the roof, and along mysterious passages hewn out of the rocks in the years gone by as the river had forced its way.

The river was still there, deep and quiet in places, rushing and gurgling in others as it fell to a new level, and the sound seemed to pervade the whole place. The guides pointed out the features of the caves, and Mary smiled when she saw the stalagmite named for the witch, for one could easily imagine the shape of it to be that of a bent old woman with a great hooked nose, and when the guide held up his lantern, the shadow cast on the wall behind was frighteningly realistic.

They explored as far as a deep, wide cavern, where the river formed a still pool to one side before flowing over a smooth ledge to fall several feet into a narrow, rock-strewn passage that led it on its way. The lights from the lanterns were reflected eerily on the damp, glistening rock faces, and Belinda shivered.

"I would not have liked to have lived here," she commented. "Is there much more?"

"They say the caves stretch for miles," one of the guides replied. "There are several passages leading from this chamber," he went on, swinging his lantern so that its beams showed the yawning entrance to one of them, "but it is not safe for you to venture farther. We must return now."

They retraced their steps for a while in silence, and then came to a narrow passage where they must go singly. One of the guides went ahead with one lantern, but as the first members of the party joined him after squeezing through the narrowest part, he had to move further along to give them room, so that the remainder were left with only the illumination of the lantern at the rear.

Teresa uttered a gasp, quickly suppressed, as the lights dimmed. She reached out and her hand came into contact with another, to which she clung tightly as she negotiated the passage.

"Can you see, Teresa?" Matthew's voice came to her, distorted by the echoes in the enclosed space, and the pressure on her hand increased.

"Yes, thank you," she whispered. "For a moment I was stupidly apprehensive."

She emerged from the narrowest part to find the way ahead illuminated only very faintly as the first guide moved on round a bend. The center of the path they were following was worn smooth, but there were uneven, rough edges and the occasional rough stone. Hurrying to catch up with the dimly perceived figures in front of her, Teresa stumbled as she caught her foot on a projection, and would have fallen had it not been for the helping hand which still held hers.

She recovered her footing and looked ahead into a blackness lightened only by a faint reflection from the lantern behind. She took a hesitant step forward, and then her companion edged alongside her. Teresa looked back. She could not distinguish the figures immediately next to her, but could hear Sir Ingram speaking and Belinda's reply. In the glow from the rear lantern she saw the faces of Paul Ward and the guide.

"The way is very narrow here," the guide commented. "Careful how you go, sir, the passage swings to the right."

"Go ahead to give us a better light," Sir Ingram suggested, and he stood to one side in the entrance to what appeared a narrow, deep cave gouged out of the rock face.

The man stepped forward to come past, treading carefully on the rough edges of the passage floor, but before he reached Teresa at the front of the group he gave a grunt of mingled pain and surprise, doubled up, and collapsed senseless to the ground, his lantern falling and its light being extinguished, leaving them in utter darkness.

Belinda screamed, and Teresa bit back a cry.

"Hold me tightly, I am following the wall," a voice whispered in her ear, and a firm, steady arm caught her round the waist and gently urged her forward.

Some yards ahead, as the rest of the party waited in a small circular chamber for the others to catch up with them, Belinda's scream erupted suddenly, startlingly, into the cave, and for a few seconds no one moved.

"Wait here, please, ladies and gentlemen," the guide said. "I will go back with the lantern."

He set off, but before he had disappeared with

the light, Mary found her arm grasped roughly by Matthew.

"Teresa—she is back there!" he told her urgently, and plunged after the guide. Startled, Mary took several steps after him, halting when the disappearing light left her in total darkness.

As she hesitated, trying to feel her way cautiously with outstretched hands, another scream, abruptly bitten off, reached them.

"Has none of you a light?" she demanded, and as she spoke the flicker of a spark answered her. In a few seconds one of the men, the brother of Teresa's friends, had lit the stub of a candle with his flint.

His cousin produced another candle stub, and Mary took it from him, smiling briefly, and before he could utter a protest, turned and followed Matthew back along the passage.

Now the sound of terrified sobbing, interspersed with less-terrified screams, came to her, and she rounded the bend in the passage to find Matthew before her, blocking the way. Peering over his shoulder, she saw Belinda huddled against the wall, while Paul Ward and Mr. Morris bent over the recumbent figure of the guide. His dropped lantern had been relit and illuminated the scene, but the other guide was nowhere to be seen.

"Matthew, what has happened? Where is Teresa?" she queried anxiously, but he did not appear to have heard her. He moved forward quickly as the sobbing continued, and Mary looked, puzzled and afraid, about her. Belinda was moaning slightly, but the sobs came from further away, and then Mary saw another faint glow to one side and realized that there was another opening, which Matthew was heading for, and she ran after him.

It was another small passage, very short and opening onto a narrow platform which ended abruptly in a jagged edge, with a deep blackness beyond it. The second guide was there, holding his lantern aloft, and Mary could see Teresa crouched on the edge of the platform, sobbing violently as she struggled with Sir Ingram, who was having some difficulty in preventing her frantic movements from sending them both over the edge into the void below.

Above the sound of Teresa's crying there was a dull roaring sound, and it took some moments before Mary's shocked senses grasped that it was the voice of the river, and that the platform looked over a deep drop into its turbulent depths.

"Teresa, my love!" Matthew exclaimed, moving towards her.

She looked up, and her sobs increased as she stretched her arms towards him. With a couple of strides he reached her, and as Sir Ingram was able to use the distraction to drag her away from the dangerous edge, Matthew bent to gather her in his arms.

"Can you persuade her to walk?" Sir Ingram

enquired coolly. "I have no fancy to carry her all the way out of here."

"I will carry you, Teresa," Matthew declared swiftly, throwing a glance of hatred at Sir Ingram.

"No, no, I can contrive, now that you are with me," Teresa gasped, struggling to her feet and attempting to control her sobs.

With Matthew's arm about her, she went slowly back along the passage. Sir Ingram gestured to the guide to follow, and looked quizzically at Mary, offering his arm.

"Unless you are afraid to remain at the rear with me?" he said softly.

"Why in the world should I be? What happened? How did Teresa come to be here?" she asked in bewilderment as she took his arm.

"She thinks I was trying to kill her," he replied unemotionally, "hence her terror as I tried to hold her safely."

"No, she could not believe such!" Mary replied, instinctively rejecting the notion. "But how did she come to be in such a place?"

Before he could answer they had reached the others, and Teresa was being bombarded with exclamations and questions from the rest of the party.

"Let us defer the explanation until we are out of here," Sir Ingram said crisply. "How is the guide?"

The man was sitting up, supported by Paul,

and he looked up at Sir Ingram, a weak smile on his face.

"I shall be better in a moment, sir," he said slowly. "Just a moment of blackness as I hit my head. But how came I to fall?"

No one answered him, for Teresa, surrounded by the others, turned and dramatically flung out her arm, pointing at Sir Ingram, while with her other hand she stroked her neck.

"He tried to strangle me!" she cried. "And push me into the river!"

Aghast, Mary stepped in front of her.

"Teresa, you are out of your mind!" she exclaimed. "How dare you make such a wicked accusation!"

"It is true!" Teresa insisted. "Keep him away from me!" she added, as Sir Ingram took a step towards her, and drew back into Matthew's protective embrace.

"As I have indicated," Sir Ingram intervened smoothly, "this is no time to discuss it."

"Indeed, let us remove from here," Mary said briskly. "Matthew, will you and Caroline take Teresa out first—the guide can light you. No, Sir Ingram, leave it to them," she ordered as he moved to pass her.

He glanced at her, his eyebrows raised, and then grinned.

"A managing female, I collect," he murmured

softly, so that only she could hear, but obediently stepped back.

She flushed, but raised her head higher. "The rest of us have several candles. Paul, can you and Mr. Morris help the other guide? Are you ready to try and move?" she went on, smiling encouragingly down at him.

He was gingerly feeling a large bruise on the side of his face, but he nodded, and with Paul's help staggered to his feet.

"Sir Ingram, be so good as to take the other lantern," Mary continued, looking at him challengingly, and then, at the expression on his face as he smiled down at her, turned hastily away and moved after the others, who were already going along the passage.

The rest of the way out of the caves passed without mishaps. They all breathed sighs of relief to reach the fresh air and see the sunlight. The girls were plying Teresa with questions, but Mary took charge and firmly bade them to leave her in peace and sent them on their way to the inn at the bottom of the valley. When they reached it, she bore Teresa off into a small private parlor the landlord quickly made ready for her, permitting only Matthew to accompany them.

"Teresa must rest in peace for a while," she declared. "Order drinks for yourselves. We will have some tea, if you please," she added to the maid hovering by the door of the parlor.

"And a brandy for me," Matthew said to the girl.

When they had been supplied and the maid had left the room, Mary looked at Teresa. She had recovered to a great extent, but lay limply back in the deep, brocade-covered armchair while Matthew sat beside her on a stool and comfortingly held her hands in his.

"Do you feel able to talk about it?" Mary said gently.

Teresa looked up at her.

"I was so terrified," she said slowly, and shivered. "It was so dark, and suddenly his hands were about my neck, and he was forcing me backward! This was no accident, Mary! Look at my neck!"

She twisted herself to show Mary the long bruises on both sides of her neck, feeling them tenderly.

"How ever did you come to be there?"

"It was dark, the first guide had disappeared, and as the second one came past Ingram, he tripped him up."

"Did you see him?" Mary asked quickly.

"No, it was too dark, I only know he was next to me because I heard him speak," Teresa replied. "It must have been him! He was holding my hand—I had thought it was you, Matthew, for when he first took it to help me in that narrow path, you spoke, and it seemed to me you were next to me."

"Well?" Mary asked, deciding to ignore this point of Teresa's behavior.

"When the guide fell, or was pushed, he—Ingram—whispered that he was following the wall, and led me on, but he took me down the other passage. Then he tried to murder me!"

"He could not have done!"

"But the marks are plain enough on Teresa's neck," Matthew put in. "Somone tried to kill her, and if not Sir Ingram, who could it have been?"

Mary stared at them for a moment. "Who else was at the back?" she said slowly. "Your friends were all with Matthew and I at the front, for they lit the candles. Caroline was there, which leaves Paul and Belinda, Sir Ingram, and Mr. Morris."

"You see!" Teresa exclaimed. "They could not have done it!"

"They were all by the guide when I reached the place," Matthew reminded Mary. "Only Sir Ingram could have been with Teresa."

"It is impossible," Mary declared, but with a slight hesitation in her voice. It must have been one of the three men, and neither Paul Ward nor Mr. Morris could have the slightest possible motive for attacking Teresa. "I cannot believe it!" she added to herself.

"Because he has been treating you courteously, enslaving you as he knows how to do only too well!" Teresa said bitterly, and Mary flushed, partly in anger, but also because she recognized the truth in what Teresa said. It was because she found Sir Ingram attractive that she found it difficult to believe ill of him.

"I shall take you away from him," Matthew promised. "He shall not harm you. We will do without his permission!"

"Matthew, how can you!" Mary exclaimed. "Whatever the rights and wrongs of this matter, I cannot believe that Sir Ingram would allow Teresa to touch her money if he disapproved of your marriage. You have not enough income to keep yourself in more than moderate comfort, so how could you support Teresa as well?"

"I'll live in a cellar with Matthew!" Teresa declared passionately.

"You cannot know what you say," Mary told her sharply. "However, this is not the occasion to discuss it. How do you feel?"

"Much calmer, Mary, and thank you for protecting me."

"I do nothing of the kind," Mary replied crossly. "Are you able to ride, or should we send for a carriage from Wells?"

"I can ride," Teresa said, standing up. "Let us go, for suddenly I am excessively hungry, and dinner is bespoken at the inn where we are to stay the night."

Despite all Mary's efforts to suppress the speculation on who could have attacked Teresa, dinner that night was an uncomfortable meal, for Teresa openly accused Sir Ingram of having attempted to strangle her. The others looked at her in dismay, but Sir Ingram merely laughed.

"You believe what you wish to," was his only comment, but Belinda immediately sprang to his defence.

"It could not have been," she declared roundly, "for he was with the rest of us until after you screamed."

"Oh, you would say so!" Teresa snapped. "You are like Mary!"

Mary cast a startled glance at Sir Ingram and saw his lips twitch in amusement. But Belinda was not to be gainsaid.

"It is true," she insisted. "When the guide fell and the light went out suddenly, I screamed and I clutched at Sir Ingram's coat. I know he was with us. It was after you screamed that he moved away, for I had been holding onto the coat, and it was then that it was pulled out of my hand!"

"It could have been Paul's coat, or Mr. Morris's," Teresa answered her.

"Sir Ingram was next to me, as we had just

been talking. Paul was too far away," Belinda explained.

That cast doubt on Sir Ingram's guilt but offered no more readily believed solution, and eventually they allowed the subject to drop. The visit to Wells Cathedral on the following day was a hurried one, for everyone was anxious to return to Bath, hoping to escape from the atmosphere of doubt and the fears and worries they could not dismiss.

7

When she and Caroline reached home, Mary found a letter awaiting her from her father, and there were also some for Caroline, so they sank into chairs with sighs of relief to read them, hoping to forget the unpleasantness of the past two days.

"Father seems to be having a most enjoyable time," Mary commented. "He writes that he has met several old friends. This break has undoubtedly been good for him. For years, since my mother's death, he has been far too absorbed in his books."

"Does he mention when he plans to return to Appleacre? Not too soon, I trust, for the treatment is of great benefit to me—and I think to you also, of a different nature. I should not wish to lose you."

"He makes no mention of it. Indeed, he has sent me another draft on his bank, so he evidently expects me to remain here for some time longer. I intend to buy that silk we saw the other day, for we go to so many parties that I need far more gowns that I ever expected."

"You may as well begin to collect your wedding clothes," Caroline said with a light laugh.

"I have not decided to accept Mr. Knowle," Mary said, frowning.

"I am aware that you procrastinate," Caroline chided her mockingly. "Tell me, you do not believe Teresa's accusation, do you?"

"I do not want to," Mary confessed slowly, "yet what other explanation can there be?"

"Either it was Paul or Mr. Morris, or Teresa imagined it all. You know how she can exaggerate the slightest incident into a great drama. I expect she wandered off in the dark, was confused, and then panicked. All due to her vivid imagination."

"She did not imagine the bruises on her neck," Mary pointed out.

"No, that I will grant you. I have been wondering about it all day, and think that she could have sustained those when she was struggling with Sir Ingram."

"Oh, is that possible?" Mary exclaimed, suddenly very much happier.

"I think it very likely. That is the explanation I shall offer, for there is no other remotely possible one."

During the next few days Mary was grateful to have this theory of Caroline's to give to their acquaintances. It was obvious, the next morning after they had returned to Bath, that the whole story of the incident, embellished with lurid detail, had been spread abroad by the others of the party. Mrs. Wright was the first to ask Mary about it.

"I heard that your brother had been found alone with Miss Standish, and that Sir Ingram attacked him," she said plainly.

"Who ever told you that, ma'am?" Mary asked, astonished.

Mrs. Wright shrugged. "I *think* I had it from Mrs. Bellamy, and she said that Lady Ferrars had told her, and she had heard it from Mr. Morris himself. Since he had been present, I wondered, though I could not truly credit the tale."

"You were right not to do so, for it is a complete fabrication!" Mary told her firmly, and gave her Caroline's explanation, stressing that Teresa and Matthew had been with the rest of the party the whole time. "Mr. Morris cannot have said such a thing, and whatever he said must have been distorted."

"You relieve my mind." Mrs. Wright smiled at her. "I could not believe it of either your brother or Sir Ingram."

"Pray do your utmost to scotch this tale," Mary begged her.

"Indeed I will, and tell them that I have it direct from you," Mrs. Wright promised.

The rumor persisted, however, and Mrs. Leigh taxed Teresa with behaving immodestly. Angrily denying it, Teresa immediately sought out Matthew, and the two of them attracted even more gossip by openly flouting the critics and escaping whenever they could from Mrs. Standish's lax chaperonage to spend their time walking together in Spring Gardens or Stanley Gardens.

Mary, concerned for Matthew, remonstrated with him, but to no avail. He protested that whatever happened, he was determined to marry Teresa, and it was better that the whole world should know. She could not bring him to see that unless he and Teresa behaved with circumspection Sir Ingram would not give his consent to their marriage. Matthew persisted in his belief that Sir Ingram had attempted to murder Teresa, and nothing would induce him to consider other explanations. In which case, he pointed out, Sir Ingram would never agree, and it was unavailing even to try to win his approval.

Eventually he took himself off to ride on the hills, and Mary hoped that the exercise would rid him of his anger, but she knew how Matthew brooded on injuries and how, when he was convinced of some matter, he could hold stubbornly to his opinion.

Sir Ingram conducted himself as though nothing untoward had occurred, and though at first some apprehensive glances were cast his way, he ignored all the hints so blandly, and gave a crashing set-down to the one matron so bold as to mention the accusation against him directly, that soon everyone was coming round to the opinion that it was all a shocking exaggeration.

Mary had not seen much of Teresa, apart from meeting her in the Pump Room, until one evening when Mrs. Leigh gave a dress party. This was to be a much grander affair than the previous one, and would include many of the new acquaintances she had made in Bath. Mary found herself to be unduly nervous as the time approached, and fussed about the arrangement of her hair in a most uncharacteristic fashion.

"I have my doubts about this gown, Caroline," she said worriedly when she was finally ready. "The neck has been cut far too low."

"Nonsense," Caroline replied. "It becomes you exceedingly well."

Indeed Mary looked very fine. The pearl-colored silk gown was elegantly trimmed with gold braid, and she carried a small painted fan and had a rope of pearls twisted in her hair, which, instead of being smoothed back as usual, had been permitted to fall in a cascade of ringlets over one pretty shoulder.

At last Caroline persuaded her that she had no cause for worry, and they drove to Great Pulteney Street. The party was already crowded, and when they were greeted by Mrs. Leigh she waved them on towards the back parlor.

"Most of the young people are there," she said cheerfully. "They are playing with that dratted parrot. He'll get so conceited there'll be even more difficulty in shutting him up!"

They laughed and went to find Teresa and many of her young friends admiring the bird.

"Aunt Hermione allows him in the drawing room when there are no guests," Teresa was explaining. "He amuses her, but she says his language is insufficiently polite for company!"

The parrot, who had been sitting preening himself, his back to the room, suddenly emitted a piercing scream, and when the deafening noise had finished, Teresa laughingly told them that he had heard one of the parlor maids, who had not realized that he was there, give such a scream when she had first encountered him.

"Pretty bird, damn bird, dandy, darling, hold your tongue, go to bed," the parrot rattled off, turning to survey his audience with a pair of glittering eyes. Then he began to yap like a dog.

"That is Carlos, one of my aunt's dogs, who detests him," Teresa said with a laugh.

"Bad dog, down, down, damn bird, go to bed, miny, miny."

"What does he say?"

"Oh, it's Aunt Hermione. Her name has defeated him."

"How long does it take to make him learn a new word?" one of the girls asked, venturing to put a finger in the cage, but withdrawing it hastily when the parrot made a snap towards it with his vicious-looking beak.

"It depends," Teresa replied. "Sometimes he begins to say something he's only heard once, and yet when I have tried to teach him a new word he sometimes utterly refuses to say it. I suppose it is what takes his fancy."

"Fancy, fancy, fancy boy," the parrot gabbled, and after a few more minutes, when Teresa considered that he had shown off sufficiently, she suggested that they might like to return to the other room, where dancing was being arranged.

They began to leave the room, and the parrot uttered a lifelike sob.

"Don't go, don't go," he pleaded, and then appeared to burst into uncontrollable tears, to the amusement of the visitors. Mary glanced swiftly at Teresa, suspecting that the parrot had learned this phrase from her, but Teresa seemed unconcerned, not in the least discomposed, and Mary hoped that no one else would think as she had.

When she walked into the other parlor she found Mr. Morris standing beside the door, and he approached her, saying that he wished to speak with her.

She permitted him to lead her to a couple of chairs near the window, wondering what he could possibly have to say. She did not like the man, and tried not to let this show in her face as she smiled at him, waiting for him to begin whatever it was he had to say.

"A most distressing affair, at Wookey," he said after a few preliminary coughs and after glancing round to see that no one else could overhear them.

"Indeed," Mary agreed briefly.

"Mrs. Standish is naturally most concerned. She fears for Teresa's life."

"Surely she does not credit the story Teresa tells? It was largely imagination."

"Oh, my dear young lady, it is clear that you do not know how very wicked the world can be. Remember that there have been other attempts on Teresa's life."

"All accidents," Mary said firmly.

He smiled and shook his head. "You choose to believe it. I can only hope that you are not proved wrong. Sir Ingram is a hard man, and determined to have his way."

"I will not believe him a murderer! Besides, what good would Teresa's death be to him? Surely her fortune would go to her mother?"

He looked quickly about him, then put finger to his lips.

"But of course," he whispered. "Dear Mrs. Standish has not yet realized that she too is in danger!"

Mary stared at him, and then laughed. "Mr. Morris, the notion is ludicrous!"

He did not seem offended. "That is what you are meant to think, but I warn you, my dear Miss Wyndham, for it seems to me that you have too great a partiality for Sir Ingram. I would not wish so charming a young lady to be hurt by such a villain!"

Mary flushed in annoyance. "I thank you for your concern, but it is unnecessary," she said coldly, and rose from her chair. Without giving him an opportunity to reply, she swept away and went impetuously from the room, intending to go to the drawing room. Outside in the hall, however, she found Matthew, and to her surprise he was talking amiably with Sir Ingram. They turned and smiled at her, and Sir Ingram raised his eyebrows.

"Why do you desert the dancing, Miss Wyndham?"

"It has not yet begun," she said, feeling foolish.

"But it will. In point of fact, I hear the musicians tuning up. Will you honor me?"

She found it most difficult to concentrate, and several of her replies were made at random. Knowing that he was laughing at her served to make her even more confused, and she was thankful to escape at the end of the dance, having been aware of Mr. Morris's gaze fixed on them, and uncomfortable when she recalled his insinuations of her partiality for Sir Ingram.

She contrived to avoid Sir Ingram for the remainder of the party, but found herself watching him much of the time and chided herself for behaving foolishly. That night she tossed and turned in bed, trying not to think of how he had danced several times with Belinda, and how the girl had sparkled up at him, laughing and teasing. Why, she demanded angrily to herself as she tried to find a cool spot on the pillow to rest her cheek, should this man have such an effect on her? Why did she constantly think of his smile, the way he had of lifting his eyebrows sardonically, his elegant figure, the deep yet clear tones of his voice? I ought to be more concerned about whether he is guilty of these attacks, if they are attacks, on Teresa, she thought, but it was of no use, for somehow that did not matter, he could not be guilty, and his image would not be banished from her thoughts.

The following morning, in the Pump Room, a rather tired and dispirited Mary met Teresa, who was glowering about her in angry, frustrated manner.

"Have you seen Matthew or Ingram?" she demanded without ceremony.

"Not this morning," Mary replied. "What has occurred to put you out of countenance?"

"Matthew, if you please, has sent me a message that he cannot ride with me this morning as we had arranged, because he prefers to go to some horrid boxing contest!"

"I am sure he did not phrase it quite like that," Mary protested, unable to restrain her laughter.

"That was the import! I remained at home, waiting for him, and all that arrives is this note. I had thought we would be free because Ingram would be out of Bath this morning."

"It really is too bad of Matthew to let you down," Mary sympathized, though she felt bound to add that they should not have been going behind Sir Ingram's back. "Has he gone alone?"

"No, with Paul Ward. But Ingram has gone too, and I *cannot* understand how Matthew can bear to be with him after the way he has treated me! Matthew talked with him last night, and afterwards seemed of the opinion that he was not so evil as he had thought before! I know that Ingram will bamboozle Matthew into liking him, as he did Godfrey, and Matthew *knows* what he is trying to do to me! I am so afraid that he will try to remove Matthew like he did Godfrey. He made friends with Godfrey and took him to all sorts of disreputable places before he killed him!"

"While I would have no desire to attend a boxing contest, it is not considered disreputable for gentlemen to go there," Mary said judiciously.

"Ingram is supposed to be an excellent boxer himself. He goes to some odious place in Jermyn Street," Teresa commented.

She then went off to join her mother, and Mary reflected that it was largely jealousy that Matthew should seek other company that had put Teresa so out of temper.

This mood persisted for the next few days, and whenever Mary saw Teresa it was to receive a string of complaints about how Matthew was neglecting her. Mary began to wonder whether he was growing tired of Teresa, but he was as vehement as ever, when next she met him, about his intention to marry her. He was less open about his feelings towards Sir Ingram, maintaining stoutly that he had accepted invitations from Paul and it was sheer chance that Sir Ingram had also been on the various expeditions. Apart from the visit to the boxing contest, it appeared that Matthew had also been introduced to the niceties of cockfighting.

"That is all he tells me of," Teresa said bitterly.

"I would not be surprised if Ingram were taking him to even worse places than that. I suspect that Ingram's latest *chère amie* is not very far away!" she added darkly.

"He surely would not take Matthew into such company!" Mary protested, her heart giving an uncomfortable lurch.

"Why not?" Teresa asked coolly. "He would think any means of detaching Matthew from me acceptable. But he shall not win! I am determined that he shall not! Do not be concerned, Mary, for your brother. I will not permit Ingram to lead him into such ways!"

Privately Mary did not think Teresa would have much success in prizing Matthew away from his new entertainments, and she discounted the more lurid of Teresa's suspicions. The next time she saw Matthew he seemed content, and told her enthusiastically about his new activities.

"I won a hundred pounds last night at cards," he informed her cheerfully.

She looked at him quickly. "Gambling now?"

"What do you mean by 'now'?" he asked, bridling slightly.

"I was concerned that you might stake more than you could afford, that is all."

"I have more wit than that," she was told loftily. "Now that I have some of the ready—and I'm willing to admit that I was almost cleaned out—I shall not play again. I need it for the next few weeks, and cannot afford to stake it again and lose it."

Mary trusted that he would hold to this resolution, but she knew that it was fatally easy for young men to imagine that they might win again and be tempted to sit down at the card tables. She considered approaching Sir Ingram and pleading with him not to encourage her brother in these pursuits, but the thought of how he would look at her, amused and slightly mocking, prevented her from making the attempt. When she chided herself with cowardice she quickly made the excuse that it would more likely have had an adverse effect in that Sir Ingram would have taken a perverse delight in tempting Matthew just to annoy her.

Yet when next she saw him she was ashamed of her suspicions, for he was exceedingly considerate. It was at a dinner party given by the Wards, and as the chairs Mary and Caroline had hired to take them to the Royal Crescent came to a stop about halfway along this magnificent terrace, Sir Ingram had appeared to hand Mary out. He had been most attentive, and even though at dinner he had been seated between her and Belinda, he did not neglect her, but divided his time scrupulously between them.

He mentioned that Matthew had been with them on several occasions.

"It gives him something to think about other than Teresa, and she can be most wearing, as I know only too well," he laughed.

"She was very frightened by what happened," Mary excused Teresa.

"Undoubtedly. Miss Wyndham, I am convinced that you do not believe the accusation she has made about me?"

Faced with this bald statement, Mary blushed, and shook her head.

"Of course I do not," she said quietly.

"I had heard of your defense of me and your explanation that it was all Teresa's imagination. Do you truly believe that?"

"I cannot— How could it be anything else?" Mary asked.

He smiled, grimly. "How, indeed. But enough of that, for I have a favor to beg of you. I am leaving Bath for two or three days, and I beg you, in so far as it lies within your powers, to insure that my foolish cousin does nothing disastrous while I am away."

Startled, Mary glanced up at him. "I do not see how I can," she murmured, "but naturally, if it were possible, I would attempt to restrain her."

"She does value your opinion," he said quietly, "and you see quite a deal of her."

After a few more remarks, he turned to Belinda, and Mary's attention was claimed by her other neighbor. When they had left the table, she had no more private speech with Sir Ingram, but found herself wondering what could be taking him away from Bath.

At some time during the evening the suggestion was made that an expedition be made into the Cotswold Hills, to the north of the town, two days later, and an alfresco meal be taken. The idea was popular, and soon there were a dozen people included, and several more, like Mrs. Standish, who wished to drive instead of ride. Arrangements were made for the food to be taken in the carriages and for everyone to meet at one of the villages six or seven miles from the town. The party finished with everyone in high good humor, concerned only that the good weather should hold for the next few days.

The day was fine, and the party was augmented by several others brought along by friends. They set off to climb Lansdown Hill, and more than twenty riders were stretched out along the road. At the top they gave their horses free rein for a while until they had galloped the freshness out of them.

After that they proceeded in a more sedate fashion, reaching the village long before those coming in the carriages. Stabling their horses at the inn, they wandered off in small groups to explore the village. Seeing that Teresa was with a group of girls and Matthew with Jonathan Wright, Mary did not consider it necessary to force her presence on either of them, so she and Caroline strolled into the church to escape from the heat of the sun.

The meal, eaten under the shade of some old oaks on the edge of the village green, was a hilarious affair, and they all vowed that the event should be repeated. Towards the end of the meal, when they were reluctantly thinking of returning to Bath, Mary noticed that Teresa was unduly silent. When they were busy packing the hampers, Mary quietly asked if she felt unwell.

"I have a headache," she admitted, "but also I am excessively angry!"

"Oh? What has occurred now?"

"Ingram!" Teresa snorted. "Before he went away yesterday, he sought me out and threatened me that if I caused any more talk he would send me to Leigh Park and forbid Matthew to come near me!"

"Gracious, what occasioned this?" Mary asked, surprised. "What talk has there been?"

"None, that is the unfair part! It was just"—and she had the grace to blush slightly—"that the day previous, Matthew had come to see me, and we were alone in the small parlor. He was so angry when he found us there, and so unreasonable, for we were doing no wrong!"

"I suppose he was worried what would be said if anyone else had learned of it," Mary commented.

"Oh, you will disapprove too!" Teresa said

pettishly. "I think I will return in the curricle with Mama."

She moved away and spoke briefly to Matthew, and he approached Mary as the riders were preparing to move away.

"I will return with Teresa and lead her horse while she rides in her mama's curricle," he explained and then, nodding briefly at Mary, went across to where Teresa sat on the ground with her mother.

Tired after their exertions, Mary and Caroline were dining at home quietly when Susan brought in a note.

"The man has just arrived and says he will wait for an answer, if you please, miss," she said, handing the note to Mary.

With a brief apology to Caroline, Mary unfolded the screw of paper and read the few words it contained.

"I will call you when I have the reply ready," she said, dismissing Susan, and when the girl had left the room she turned angrily to Caroline.

"They appear to have given us the slip!" she exclaimed.

"Who? What is it?"

"A note from Mrs. Standish to ask whether Teresa is still with us! It seems that she did not drive home with her mama after all! She and Matthew must have planned it so that they could steal a few hours together. The fools! This will not endear them to Sir Ingram if he hears of it, especially after what he said!"

"Could they have eloped again?" Caroline asked worriedly.

"They have nowhere to go, and I cannot think it of them! No doubt they have been so engrossed in one another that they have forgot the time. I had best go round to Great Pulteney Street and tell them what I know. I cannot do so in a note."

"Shall I come too?" Caroline offered, but Mary saw that she was looking tired, and had a crease between her eyes.

"No, you have a headache, I fear."

"Only a slight one, nothing like the ones I used to get, I assure you," Caroline protested.

"You could do no more than I, and so it would be wiser for you to go to bed."

So saying, she went to fetch a shawl and joined the man who had brought the note, one of Mrs. Leigh's footmen.

"I must come and see Mrs. Standish," she told him. "Can you obtain a chair for me?"

He was soon back with one, and Mary was carried swiftly through the town and across the bridge, to be greeted by a distraught Mrs. Standish as she entered the house in Great Pulteney Street.

"Oh, my dear, she is not with you?" she asked, clutching at Mary's arm.

Mary was surprised at her anxiety, for she did not normally fret over Teresa's starts.

"She told me that she was planning to drive back with you, ma'am," she explained.

"Oh, the wicked one! She did stay a little behind the others, for she had been telling me some story about one of her friends, but then she and your brother set off after you, not more than a couple of hundred yards behind. They must have slipped off when they were out of our sight."

"Easily done, for there were a good many trees to provide cover," Mary said ruefully. "I should have stayed with her or spoken to you about her plans, but when I saw her remain with you when we set off, I thought no more about her."

"She deceived us both," Mrs. Standish lamented.

"And you both ought to know Teresa well enough by now not to be taken in by her tricks," a new voice contributed, and with a start Mary looked up to find Sir Ingram surveying them sardonically from the top of the stairs.

"Do pray come up to the drawing room, Miss Wyndham," he went on smoothly, before she was able to recover from the shock of seeing him. "I cannot imagine why my dear aunt keeps you standing in the hall."

"I am too distraught to know what I am doing," that lady exclaimed, nevertheless taking Mary's arm and urging her up the stairs, and towards the door that Sir Ingram held open for them.

"Have they eloped yet again?" Sir Ingram asked Mary, and she flushed angrily at his tone.

"I cannot think it, for they have nowhere to go," she retorted. "I have no doubt that they have simply forgot the time."

"I have not your delightfully innocent trust in people," he commented lazily.

Stung into a retort, she faced him angrily. "Teresa is displaying greater constancy than you predicted! They seem very much in love, and it is natural for them, fearing to be forcibly separated at any moment, to endeavor to spend all the time they can together!"

"You would defend them? And what makes you think there will be any forcible separation? You imply, I take it, that I shall be the instrument of that separation?"

"Is that not what you intend if there is no natural ending to the affair?" she demanded hotly. "Is not this threat to send her away an excuse for this? If they show that they are determined to be faithful to one another, can you truthfully say that you would approve? Matthew is poor, I will admit, by your standards, but you have always considered him beneath Teresa and spurned him as a possible husband for her!"

"Not for what you assume to be my reasons," he replied mildly. "Teresa will not be happy if she has a husband who cannot control her, and neither, believe me, would that husband! Could you wish that fate on your brother?"

Mary was silent, knowing that what he said

was probably true but unwilling to admit that her brother would be unable to manage Teresa if they were married.

"Oh, do stop this useless argument!" Mrs. Standish cried. "Where is my Teresa? For all you care, Ingram, she might be lying dead somewhere, attacked again as she has been so many times! Why am I alone when it happens? Aunt Hermione is out, even Rodney is not to be found!"

"Where is he?" Sir Ingram inquired.

"Oh, at some card party, but what does it matter? *You* are here now. Why do you not organize a search party? You must do something!"

"Would you have me advertise to the whole town that she is missing in the company of Mr. Wyndham?" he asked coldly, and Mrs. Standish, after staring helplessly at him for a moment, burst into hysterical tears.

"What shall I do?" she moaned in between her gasping sobs.

"I would suggest that you go to bed," he advised sharply. "If she has not come in soon, I will myself ride out to make inquiries. Aunt Hermione should be back from her dinner party soon, and then I will leave you in her charge."

Mrs. Standish began to urge that he start at once, when the door opened and the culprits walked into the room.

8

"*Where have you been?* Oh, you wicked girl, causing me all this worry! How dare you!" Mrs. Standish greeted Teresa.

"Mama, do not be disturbed, I have come to no harm. Oh, so you are back, Ingram? It is you upsetting Mama, is it? This time, Mama dear, it was a *real* accident. It was simply that my horse cast his shoe and we had to walk some way before we could find a smithy. That is all, and I am sorry that you have been worried, but there was no need, for Matthew takes very good care of me!"

She looked challengingly at Sir Ingram, a smile playing on her lips. He returned her look unsmilingly.

"Why did you tell me that you intended to drive home with your mother?" Mary put in, angry at the air of nonchalance Teresa displayed.

"Mary! Forgive me, I did not realize that you were here. I am most truly sorry, but I suddenly felt better and changed my mind. We set off after you, but before we could come up to you the horse cast his shoe, as I have said. Did you all imagine that we had eloped again? Was *that* what put you all into such a pucker?"

She laughed, but kept a wary eye on Sir Ingram. Matthew had not uttered a word, but looked decidedly uncomfortable, glancing across at Mary from time to time as Teresa made her explanation.

"I thought that you might have raised some money by selling your pearls, and eloped again while Ingram was away," Mrs. Standish explained in her turn. "My precious darling, I have been so set about with anxiety. You cannot understand what a mother feels!"

"You may explain that to her later, Aunt Cecy. I propose now to escort Miss Wyndham home. Thank you for coming in response to my aunt's note, Miss Wyndham, and I regret that it was necessary to trouble you. Mr. Wyndham, will you be so kind as to call on me in my lodgings tomorrow morning? Miss Wyndham, shall we go?"

Unable to think of a way of refusing his offer, Mary uttered brief good-byes to the others, noting with some satisfaction that Matthew had paled at the last words of Sir Ingram, and passed out of the room. A footman was sent round to the mews to order Sir Ingram's curricle, and within a few minutes it was outside the front door. They had waited in an uneasy silence, and Mary did not speak other than to murmur her thanks as Sir Ingram handed her up into the vehicle.

"You need not come, Grant," he said to the groom, and he shook the reins, holding the horses in to a walk as they crossed Laura Place.

"I had thought that you would have had greater influence with your brother and my cousin, and persuaded them to behave with more decorum," he remarked conversationally a few minutes later.

Mary gasped at this attack. "I am aware that I allowed them to fool me today," she retorted swiftly, "but I am not nursemaid to either of them! Matthew is of age and does what he chooses. As for Teresa, I do not see how *I* can be expected to exercise any control over her when her mother is present!"

"Softly! I did not say control, rather influence. Teresa likes you, and I hoped, as I said at the Wards' dinner the other evening, that you might be able to guide her, be an example. You must confess that my dear Aunt Cecy is hardly the woman to have a good influence on her daughter, or even to be able to control her! I felt that I could depend on you to exert yourself on her behalf. She needs help."

"Well, I have tried and failed, and do not see what else I might have done today," Mary said angrily. "I am not her keeper, and while you refuse to permit a proper betrothal between her and my brother I cannot feel that I have any right to attempt to influence her beyond the rights of friendship!"

"But if you were to be connected to her by marriage? You would consider you had the right?" he asked smoothly.

"Since that eventuality seems remote after what they have done to annoy you, I cannot see the purpose of such speculation. Besides, she would then be Matthew's responsibility," Mary replied. "She is now yours, at any event, not mine!"

"Then I must see what I can do," he commented, and Mary suspected angrily that he was laughing at her.

They reached Queen Square and he halted the curricle outside the house.

"Can you jump down? I cannot leave the horses."

Mary disdained the hand he held out to assist her and sprang lightly down, turning to thank him coldly for having seen her home.

"I shall no doubt see you tomorrow," he replied. "Good night and thank you for what you have tried to do for my wretched cousin."

The door had been opened, and Mary did not reply to this, but nodded and went into the house to find that Caroline had retired to bed and was asleep. There was no one with whom she could discuss Teresa's latest escapade, and she tossed and turned in bed for half the night before dropping into a troubled sleep that left her heavy-eyed and with a headache the following morning, so that she pleaded this as an excuse not to go out but to remain quietly at home.

Caroline returned from her morning treatment earlier than usual to see whether Mary was well enough to go that evening to a dance at the Assembly Rooms.

"By the way, I have asked Jonathan to escort us tomorrow," she added.

"To escort us?" Mary asked blankly.

"Yes, to visit Mr. Knowle. Had you forgot that tomorrow was the day we had planned for the visit? Of course, if you do not feel quite the thing, we could send our excuses."

"No, I must not cry off, that would be unpardonable. Oh, dear, but it had completely slipped from my memory! How dreadful!"

"I saw Matthew briefly," Caroline went on, "and he begged that if we could arrange for another escort, we would excuse him. Jonathan was only too willing to oblige me when he realized that he would thereby spend most of the day in your company!"

Mary frowned. "You imagine it," she replied shortly. "Was Matthew in a very bad humor?"

"A mite embarrassed, naturally, after yesterday's prank. I was puzzled, to be honest, for he seemed to have an air of excitement about him. He had just been talking with Sir Ingram before he came across to me. You do not think that he has relented, do you?"

"I would hardly expect it, after his attitude last night. I expect Matthew has thought up something else to annoy us! Well, I have washed my hands of the whole business and he can do as he pleases!" Mary declared.

Nonetheless, intrigued to see how her brother conducted himself after what she had assumed would be an awkward interview that morning, she observed him with some interest that evening. He did not seem to behave any more circumspectly than usual towards Teresa, judging by the way he made straight for her side, when he entered the ballroom, and remained with her for some time before reluctantly coming to pay his respects to Mary and Caroline.

"We went to a bang-up race this afternoon," he said boyishly after greeting them and seeing that Mary did not intend to reprove him. "Sir Ingram took me, for it was a private affair, and he knew one of the fellows taking part. His friend won, too!"

"You seem on better terms with him," Mary said, smiling. "Does that mean that he has forgiven you and begins to favor your suit?"

Matthew looked embarrassed. "He's making an

effort to be pleasant," he admitted, "but he will not discuss Teresa."

"Do you still think him capable of what Teresa suspects?" Mary asked, lowering her voice.

"It's difficult to, but what other explanation can there be?" Matthew replied, looking troubled. "I do not know what to believe!"

It was left at that, for Paul Ward then appeared to ask Mary to dance, and when they had finished neither Teresa nor Matthew was visible. Sir Ingram had arrived, however, and he soon approached Mary and asked for the next dance.

"I am gaining a better impression of your brother," he said abruptly as he led her onto the floor.

Mary looked up at him. "Just because he has some tastes that are similar to your own?" she asked quickly, and he laughed.

"Not solely for that reason. He stood up to me in an admirable fashion this morning. No, I have hopes that he might after all be capable of controlling my dear cousin. He is not so infatuated as I thought, and that bodes well, for she will respect him the more."

"Does that mean that you will give your permission?" Mary asked hopefully.

He looked down at her and smiled, so that he heart performed acrobatics and left her breathless.

"Not necessarily," he replied slowly, then grinned. "I am loath to abandon my role as the wicked cousin. Although," he went on as Mary flashed him a startled look, "Teresa is either remarkably daring or exceedingly foolhardy, if she really believes in her own theories!"

Mary laughed, uncertainly. "She exaggerates, I am sure, and does not truly believe what she says," she murmured.

"She permits her imagination to run riot, and dramatizes unmercifully. But I shall not relent merely to disprove her fantasies."

"Then what do you mean to do?"

He smiled, disturbingly. "I may need to keep it as a bribe," he said softly. "Come, let me procure you a drink."

Wondering what he had meant, Mary allowed him to lead her through to the tea room, and she was soon settled at a table with the refreshments he had obtained for her.

"How are you enjoying Bath?" he asked as he sat down beside her.

"Enormously, apart from Matthew and Teresa," she said frankly, and he laughed delightedly.

"Precisely my own sentiments! How much longer do you propose remaining?"

"I am not sure. My father may be returning to Appleacre soon, although I am not certain when, and he will need me when he does. Caroline is so much better that she may soon be able to go home, and then of course I would go too. Which occurs first I cannot say!"

"Do you never act to please yourself?"

She looked up at him, expecting mockery, but she could not read the expression in his eyes.

"Frequently," she assured him, "but I do not see how my return home could be described so! This visit was made expressly to help Caroline, and it happened to suit my father for me to be away. It has suited me too!"

"Despite Matthew and Teresa! Miss Wyndham, there is so much to be discussed, and here is not the place! Will you drive out with me tomorrow morning?"

Surprised, but assuming that he meant to talk farther about Matthew and Teresa, she accepted, and then recalled that she was engaged to drive out to visit Mr. Knowle.

"Oh, dear, I cannot tomorrow," she said, and explained.

"The day afterwards then," he suggested easily and, when she agreed, promised to call for her at her lodgings. Then he talked about some of their Bath acquaintances, retailing many anecdotes and providing her with much amusement.

Leading her back into the ballroom, he danced with her again and then, when she was claimed by another partner, went to talk with Caroline and a group of her friends. Afterwards he disappeared, for when Mary looked again he was nowhere to be seen.

Teresa was in an excited mood, bubbling over

with high spirits, and Mary noticed that Matthew seemed to be paying her as much attention as ever before. That probably accounted for her air of satisfaction, Mary decided, and hoped that, since Sir Ingram seemed to be on the point of relenting, they would not do something idiotic to offend him.

Mary was in a happier frame of mind than she had enjoyed for some time. Caroline had observed her dancing with Sir Ingram and noted the long time she had been with him in the tea room, but discreetly avoided any direct reference to it.

"Oh, Jonathan gave me his apologies, for he cannot accompany us tomorrow," she said as they reached home. "It was something his mother had arranged that he would do, and he was most put out. But it did not matter. Sir Ingram was there, and offered to come to his stead. I hope you do not object?"

For some reason Mary was most reluctant to accept his escort on the visit they were to make, but she could not give any satisfactory reason for her instinctive recoil, and had to assure Caroline that he would be welcome.

Caroline, who had seen the gleam of unholy amusement in Sir Ingram's eyes when he had made the offer, had difficulty in schooling her own countenance to a becoming gravity when she observed Mary's embarrassment. She wondered what the following day would bring for her friend, but, as they were to start early, recommended that they go to bed at once, so there was no discussion.

On the following morning the chaise that they had hired was bowling out of the town, with Sir Ingram riding beside it, before most of the visitors had risen from their beds.

Mr. Knowle was awaiting them when they drew up before a large, commodious rectory, set beside an old, squat, towered church on one side of the village green. To the right side of the green was the entrance to the manor house, which could be glimpsed through a thin belt of trees, and cottages sprawled round the other two sides, with half a dozen or so more substantial houses, rather similar to the one Mary lived in at Appleacre, clustered at the farthest point from the church.

Mr. Knowle had stared for a moment with undisguised hostility at Sir Ingram when the latter had dismounted and held out his hand, but then had pulled himself together and greeted him politely.

"A delightful setting, is it not?" Mr. Knowle asked proudly as they stood and surveyed the village. "The squire is an educated man, very intent on doing his best for all his tenants, and there are some agreeable people living here. Altogether a most felicitous place in which to live."

They duly registered their admiration and then

were taken into the drawing room, a spacious, comfortable chamber, to partake of the wine and cakes Mr. Knowle's housekeeper had provided. She was a plump, friendly woman, and she eyed Mary with especial curiosity, causing Mary much discomfort as she wondered whether Mr. Knowle had hinted at his hopes, or whether the woman had merely drawn her own conclusions from this visit.

After they had rested, Mr. Knowled took them on a tour of the house, expounding on its comforts in a fashion which, as Caroline said afterwards, would have done credit to a man endeavoring to sell the place.

"Which I suppose he was," she added thoughtfully.

Later they strolled into the gardens, and while they were walking through the shrubbery along a path that led to the church, Mr. Knowle slowed his pace, allowing Caroline and Sir Ingram, who had gone on in front of them, to pass out of earshot. Then he broached the subject that Mary had been expecting with some dread.

"Now that you have seen my new home, my dear Mary, I trust that it will assist you in coming to a decision. You must admit that it is a most pleasing situation, and there is some very select company in the neighborhood. Apart from the inhabitants of these houses you see across the green, there are several good families within a few miles, and they have all made me very welcome. You would not lack for agreeable friends, and neither, I venture to suggest, would your father if he also made his home with us."

In an unusually despondent mood, Mary was tempted to take the easiest way and forget the qualms that had kept her from accepting Mr. Knowle's proposal before. She knew that he would be kind, attentive to her comfort and that of her father, and it was certainly a pleasant home he had to offer her. There would be no more problems if she accepted him, and she longed to forget her worries and doubts and Matthew's reprehensible behavior. It was tempting to think of placing her burdens on shoulders that she knew would willingly bear them. "But I do not love him," a tiny voice persisted, and somehow Mary wondered whether, as Mr. Knowle had asserted, love was bound to develop after they were married. It was a risk that she was reluctant to take, but she knew that she had no right to try his patience for much longer.

She sighed and tried to explain some of this to him. He made light of her fears, saying that love before marriage was a sin, and naturally she would not allow herself to indulge in such thoughts or feelings.

"If you did, my dear, I would not respect you as I do, and certainly not consider you a fit wife for a clergyman! Allow me to be the judge. If you have no personal revulsion to me and think that we could be friends, as indeed I hope we are already, then love will come and be sanctified after marriage."

"I feel that I am taking an unconscionable time," Mary apologized.

"I am patient, for I know that this is a most serious decision. But now you have seen the house and can soon come to a decision. I have to be in Bath on Saturday, two days from now. Shall I wait on you then?"

Mary grasped at this slight reprieve. "You are too good to me," she said slowly, and took a deep breath. "I will give you a definite answer then, I promise."

He seemed content, and the remainder of the visit passed uneventfully. Mr. Knowle was in an almost jovial mood, and Mary endeavored to appear lighthearted. She was very silent as they drove home, however, and merely smiled when, at parting, Sir Ingram promised to call for her on the following morning. She was chiding herself for not having had the courage to give a firm decision immediately. How would the delay of yet two more days help her to make up her mind? she wondered, for nothing could change, and perhaps her scruples were silly and he was correct in saying that love would come.

Caroline, with her suspicions of what had been said and silent relief that apparently Mary had not yet accepted Mr. Knowle, judged it more discreet to avoid the topic until Mary herself should introduce it. She praised the house and the village, but added that Bath was just a little too far for easy access, and Bristol, about the same distance away, not a great deal better.

"Mr. Knowle will not be able to plan for visits to London very easily, with what appears to be a large parish to care for. He has no curate to assist him, and from what he told me he does not intend to have one."

She then began to talk of their plans for the next few days, dwelling on her delight that Arthur would be able to join her soon for a short visit.

"I have never before been away from him for more than a few days, usually when he has had to go to London on business, and I had not realized how truly lonely I would be," she confessed. "Oh, you have been a great comfort to me, Mary, but I loved Arthur the moment I saw him, and when we are apart I never cease thinking of him."

Would she ever feel like that about Mr. Knowle, Mary wondered, and, unbidden, the image of Sir Ingram came into her mind. Inexplicably she felt her spirits rising as she thought of their drive on the following day.

Sir Ingram arrived promptly. Caroline had already departed for her treatment, and Mary was ready, so that she was able to go down as soon as

Sir Ingram was announced. His groom held the horses' heads while Sir Ingram, looking appreciatively at Mary's walking dress of soft blue muslin, edged with narrow rolls of a slightly darker shade, handed her up into the curricle, a sporty affair, and then leapt up after her.

"You can walk home, Grant," he ordered, and turned the horses to drive out of the square. He had gone but a few yards, however, when to Mary's horror she saw Teresa, wild-eyed, hatless, and apparently terrified, running into the square, oblivious alike of the traffic and the disapproving looks of passers by.

"Mary, oh stop!" she cried as she saw Mary in the curricle, and veered across the roadway in front of them so that Sir Ingram, cursing under his breath, only just avoided her.

Mary sprang down from the curricle and took the distraught girl into her arms.

"My dear, be calm. What in the world has happened?"

"Mama fell down the stairs last night," Teresa gasped, trying to regain her breath.

"Oh, dear, is she badly hurt?" Mary asked in dismay.

"No, no, of course not," Teresa managed to say. "It's my parrot! He's been killed, stabbed! Oh, Mary, it's horrible!"

Mary cast a look of appeal at Sir Ingram and, since his groom, seeing the commotion, had run back to hold the horses, he came across to where Teresa clung to her.

"What is all this about the parrot?" he asked, puzzled. "who in the world would want to stab a bird?"

Teresa shrank away from him. "You should know! How could you! And it's not only the parrot, it's Mama as well now," she concluded breathlessly.

"I had best get her indoors," Mary said apologetically, and Sir Ingram nodded.

Mary put her arm about Teresa's waist and urged her towards the house. Teresa permitted herself to be led, but protested hysterically when Sir Ingram appeared to be following them in.

"No! Mary, don't let him come in! I will not have it! I'll run away, he must not come in!"

"I'm sorry. I will see that she is taken home when she is calmer," Mary promised. "I will not be able to come with you now, I am sorry."

"I might have known that morning was not the most favorable time," he remarked, and Mary gave him a puzzled look. Then he laughed slightly. "Can you manage her? I will go round to Great Pulteney Street now and find out what is amiss," he said quietly so that Teresa could not hear him, and as Mary nodded he turned away.

Mary took the distraught Teresa into their sitting room and tried to persuade her to sit down, saying that she must calm herself before trying to explain. Instead Teresa flung herself, sobbing violently, into Mary's arms.

"He did it, I know he did!" she gasped.

"My dear, do sit down," Mary said gently. "We will have some tea first."

She rang for Susan and asked her to bring tea as swiftly as possible. Teresa had flung herself into a chair, and was still crying with complete abandon, so Mary sat quietly, stroking her hand and helping her to recover from her distressing experience. Soon Susan appeared with the tea, and when she had set it down on a small table Mary dismissed her and proceeded to pour out the tea.

"Drink this," she said, offering the cup to Teresa.

Teresa stared uncomprehendingly for a moment, and then her eyes widened with terror. She sprang up and, before Mary realized her intention, pushed the cup away so that the tea spilled over the carpet.

"Really, Teresa!" Mary exclaimed, looking in amazement at the girl.

"He's poisoned the tea, he's poisoned it! Why should he smile when he left me here, where I thought I was safe?" Teresa sobbed, and then her cries rose into a scream and she flung herself back into the chair, rocking herself from side to side and plucking feverishly at her gown.

For a moment Mary was too surprised to move, but then, recalling that the best way to halt hysteria was to slap the patient hard, she dealt Teresa a stinging slap on her cheek.

Teresa gulped, stared in astonishment at Mary, and then collapsed into tears, but this time they were normal sobs, not the wild hysterics of a moment before.

"You hit me!" she gasped at last.

"I was forced to, my dear, for you were beyond yourself. Now we will drink some tea. There is nothing wrong with it, I assure you. It will help you to feel better."

Mary drank from her cup, and reluctantly Teresa followed her example.

"Now, calmly, dearest, tell me when the parrot was discovered?"

"This morning," Teresa contrived to say with more calm. "I did not go to see him when we got home last night, and this morning when I went in he was lying on the floor of the cage, horribly still! When I picked him up, he was stiff and cold!" She shuddered convulsively and Mary held her tightly.

"Poor Teresa, what a shocking discovery to have made. But why do you think he was stabbed? Could he not have died naturally?"

"There were a few spots of blood on the floor of the cage, and when I looked closer, beneath his feathers, I saw the hole! It was quite large and went right through him! It must have been something very sharp!" she wept.

"And what is this about your mama? Is she hurt?"

"Oh, no, but she is complaining as much as though her leg were broken!" said her dutiful daughter. "That happened last night, just before we got home. I had been out with Aunt Hermione to visit one of her friends. Mama did not come because she had a headache. She said that she had been unable to sleep and was going to the drawing room to fetch her new novel, and slipped. She did not fall far and has only a few bruises. I believe that Ingram pushed her!" she concluded dramatically.

Mary was shocked. "How could he?" How could he have been in the house? He was with us all day."

"But not so late. You returned soon after dark, did you not?"

Mary agreed, and Teresa, now anxious to tell her story, went on quickly, her tears forgotten.

"He has a key to the house and could have let himself in without the servants knowing," she explained.

"Yes, but why should he wish to do such a horrid thing?"

"If he cannot marry me—and Matthew made it plain to him that we do not intend to give way—then Mama is as much a hindrance to him as I am," Teresa explained patiently. "I think he has decided to murder her first and then he will turn to me. He must have killed the parrot because he—the bird—may have made a noise when Mama fell, or he thought the servants would go into that room if they heard it. He must have slipped in there after pushing Mama," she said. "Mary, I'm afraid!"

"I am not surprised, after such a dreadful thing happening, but I still cannot believe it was your cousin."

"He's getting round you now! I saw him making up to you at the Assembly Rooms, and then he went with you yesterday, and was going to take you for a drive this morning. But who else *could* it be? None of the servants would do such a thing, and there is no one who could enter the house apart from Ingram!"

"Might it have been a burglar? You do not know that it happened precisely when your mother fell, and that could have been an accident. A burglar might have got in later and been afraid when the parrot began to make a noise."

"No. The windows are all seen to early every evening. Aunt Hermione is *most* particular about that, and there are none broken that a burglar could have used. We checked that at once. No, whoever did it *must* have come through the front door, unknown to the servants, and that leaves only Ingram!"

"What does your mother say?"

"She is concerned only with her own fall! And

Aunt Hermione tells me not to be ridiculous, but she can find no other explanation!"

"I confess that it baffles me too," Mary said slowly.

"Mary, what can I do? He will succeed in the end!"

Perturbed, Mary tried to reassure her and partially succeeded in making her believe that much of what had happened to her could be explained away partly as accidents, and that it was difficult to contrive a murder in such a fashion, so that she only had to be on her guard to foil further attempts.

"What of the attack in the caves?"

"Your imagination, I am sure," Mary said firmly, but she could not devise any satisfactory explanation for this latest outrage.

Teresa was somewhat comforted, however, and after some time agreed to return home. Thinking that it would calm her, Mary suggested that they walk, and mentioned that she needed to make some purchases in Milsom Street. By the time these errands had been satisfactorily made, Teresa was chattering in a manner more akin to her normal behavior, and Mary breathed a sigh of relief. When they reached Great Pulteney Street, Teresa turned impulsively to her.

"You are so good to me! Thank you, dearest Mary! You are the nicest sister I could hope for!"

"Well, I am sure that we will one day become sisters," Mary replied, amused and pleased that Teresa seemed to have recovered from the unpleasantness of the morning. "Now that you are safely here, I will go and find Caroline."

"And I will take the dogs for a walk in Sydney Gardens," Teresa said pensively. "I am sorry that I spoiled your drive," she added, as though having just recalled the fact that she had interrupted Mary. "That is, if you really wished to go. I think it would be wiser if you were not alone with him. After all, if he can kill an innocent parrot as well as attempting to kill Mama and me, what is to stop him from killing you too? Please take great care of yourself, Mary!"

Mary smiled. "Even if your suspicions are correct, and I cannot think that they are, for what possible reason could he wish to kill me?" she demanded.

Teresa shrugged. "He had no reason to kill the parrot, and so he must be mad. In which case there is no knowing *what* he might do!"

Unable to reason with her, Mary departed, to find that Caroline had left the Pump Room and gone home. Caroline had heard all about the affair from Mrs. Leigh.

"What a macabre thing to have done," she said, shivering. "Was Teresa very deeply upset? Mrs. Standish had remained at home, and Teresa must have left the house without her knowledge."

Mary explained. "Was Mrs. Standish greatly hurt?"

"Not really, but I understand from Mrs. Leigh that she is so annoyed that she is determined to go away from Bath for a few days, to have peace and quiet to calm her overset nerves, she said. I believe she plans to visit a friend who lives in Gloucestershire."

"Did she make any reference to having been pushed? Could she fear it?"

"Mrs. Leigh did not say anything to give me that notion."

Mary explained Teresa's suspicions, and Caroline shook her head.

"The girl is nonsensical."

"If Mrs. Standish feared that she was in danger, it would explain her wish to get away."

"It seems most unlikely. Poor Mary, your drive ruined, and having to deal with an hysterical Teresa into the bargain! Never mind, no doubt Sir Ingram will repeat his invitation."

"Teresa advised me that it would be wise to avoid him," Mary said with a slight laugh. "I am likely to be his next victim, in her view."

Caroline chuckled. "Not of murder, I would have thought."

"What do you mean now?"

Caroline smiled enigmatically. "When did Mr.

Knowle say that he proposed to visit Bath?" she asked.

Mary blinked. "Mr. Knowle?" Then she recalled that she had promised an answer to that faithful lover and blushed, for she had continuously pushed the unwelcome decision to the back of her mind.

"I believe you have forgotten all about the man," Caroline challenged her.

"Well, this morning rather a lot has been happening," Mary excused herself. "Oh, dear, he comes tomorrow! And I still have not made up my mind!"

"There is not a great deal of time left, then," Caroline said, and laughed when Mary said that indeed she would have to hurry, but refused to explain the reason for her laughter.

9

At that moment Susan came in with the letters. Caroline retired to her bedchamber to read the one from Arthur, and Mary sat down with one from her father. He was a poor correspondent, and she had not expected another letter from him for some time. Then the thought occurred to her that he might be unwell, or planning to return to Appleacre, so that the letter was a summons home. Swiftly she broke the seals and unfolded the single sheet.

Mr. Wyndham began by saying how interesting he found Oxford, and Mary breathed a sigh of relief that at least he was well. Then, after digressing about Mary's visit to Bath, he suddenly changed the subject.

* * *

As you are now so well provided for, my dear child, I feel free at last to do what I have for long had in mind, delaying only because you gave me consolation for the loss of your dear mother, and because you had not yet found a home of your own to go to. That latter consideration at least no longer applies, and I have arranged with my friend Mr. Drake that I will sell the house at Appleacre and come to join him here at Oxford. When all the details of your approaching marriage are settled, and naturally you will wish to be married from our home, my plans can be made. I will hold myself ready to return home whenever it is convenient to you, but of course Mrs. Grafton's treatment must be completed first, and I know that you will not care to desert her. It only remains for me to wish you every happiness, and the joy that your dear mother and I found together. I know that you will not have your head turned if I tell you that he is the most fortunate man alive to have won your love.

There was more, but Mary hardly took it in, for it was about his doings at Oxford. What had led him to write in such a fashion? she wondered distractedly. Had Mr. Knowle allowed him to believe that she had accepted him? If so, that was an impertinence on Mr. Knowle's part, and Mary grew angry at the thought and determined that she would let him know what she thought of such pretension.

It was then that she recalled what her father had said about wishing for a long time to settle in Oxford. It was ironic that she had been protesting to Caroline that her father needed her, when all the time, it seemed, he had been patiently waiting for her to find herself a husband so that he could retreat to join his old friends. Why had he never told her that this was his wish? she wondered, and then realized that he might have feared that if she had known, she would have taken the first opportunity of marriage so as to allow him his freedom.

A sudden bleakness descended on her as she realized the implications. Her father was pleased, not only for her but that he could change his way of life. If she refused Mr. Knowle after all, it would destroy that happiness, and her father might never find it possible to retire to Oxford, for that would depend on whether she found a husband.

"I shall have to accept him," she whispered to herself, admitting at last that she did not in the least wish to do so. Trying to be calm and thinking rationally about it, she asked herself why this decision, forced on her in such a way, should cause her such distress when she had been half prepared to take it for herself a few days before.

"I like Mr. Knowle, and have known him for a long time, and we *are* friends," she told herself slowly. "Is love so important? Is it as he says, that it will come? Yet Caroline disagrees with him, and she knows what it is to marry the man she loves."

Her argument with herself went on for a long time, returning always to the fact that she did not love Mr. Knowle in the way she had felt she would want to love the man she was prepared to marry.

"But this is ridiculous!" she said eventually, rising impatiently from the chair where she had been sitting. "I have no choice and *must* accept him! There is no alternative if Papa is not to be disappointed, and that must not be! I do like Mr. Knowle, and must do as he says and trust him, and there is no purpose in thinking any more about it!"

So decided, she walked quickly to where the writing desk stood and opened it with the intention of penning a note to her father, but at that moment Caroline walked back into the room.

"What is amiss?" she asked in quick concern as she saw Mary's worried expression. "Is it your father? Is he ill?"

"No, he is well, but you had best read this," she said slowly, offering her friend the letter.

Caroline was not certain whether to be amused

or worried at the dilemma in which Mary found herself.

"And you have been saying for years that you could not leave your father and discouraging any man who showed the slightest interest in you, while all the time he has been patiently wishing you married," she said indignantly. "But you do not have to allow this to influence you with regard to Mr. Knowle," she added quickly. "You will always be welcome to make your home with us!"

"Caroline, I could not!" Mary protested, overwhelmed at this generosity.

"Well, I might not offer it if I thought that you might be there for years," Caroline chuckled. "I know that I would lose you in a few months!"

"Yes, when in despair I accepted Mr. Knowle after all—if he would wait so long," Mary retorted, refusing to consider any other implication in Caroline's remarks. "You have told me often enough that I have been unfair to him, refusing to give him a definite answer, and now that I have decided, you try to persuade me to keep him waiting for yet longer!"

"But it is the wrong answer!" Caroline almost wailed. "Oh, why did Teresa have to come rushing to you! Wretched girl!"

Reminded of the events of the morning, Mary became grave.

"I do not see how that has anything to do with

it!" she said shortly. "The poor girl must have been terrified. She was hysterical with the shock of what happened. I think I will send round a note to ask if there is any more that I can do. Possibly Mrs. Leigh would like me to visit her this evening if she still feels low."

She did this, and a reply was brought back to thank her, but Mrs. Leigh did not need her assistance. Teresa was still most distressed at the death of her parrot but seemed to have overcome her fears, with the help, Mrs. Leigh admitted, of a visit from Mr. Wyndham that seemed to do her a great deal of good. Instead, she had asked for a dose of laudanum, and said that she intended to retire early, hoping to sleep for a long time to recover from the shock.

Relieved that Teresa seemed to be behaving sensibly, Mary allowed Caroline to bully her into attending a small party that they had been invited to that evening. She had been intending to remain at home, resolving on her answer to Mr. Knowle, but after her father's letter there was little she could do other than accept him, and she agreed to go with Caroline, hoping that it would take her mind off what she knew was an unwelcome decision.

The party was at a house belonging to some friends of Mrs. Wright, and Mary had met them only once. When she and Caroline reached the house, they discovered that the Wrights were almost the only people they knew well, although they had been introduced briefly to some of the others and had seen yet more about the town, or in the Pump Room, where all the visitors to Bath were to be found at some time.

In new company Mary was able to relax, and in the interest of talking with comparative strangers she forgot her own troubles. Caroline grinned at her appreciatively when she heard one of the young men asking Mary to walk with him in Spring Gardens on the following morning.

"Mr. Knowle is not the only man who is attracted to you, you see," she pointed out with a laugh as they made their way home. "Did you accept his invitation?"

"How could I when I am expecting Mr. Knowle to call?" Mary asked, a trifle sharply.

"Oh, Mary, you do not have to accept him!" Caroline cried, but Mary would not give her friend the satisfaction of taking her advice.

"I must. I will in the end, I know, so why not now? In any event, I have promised him an answer, and the poor man deserves some consideration. He has been most patient."

Reluctantly Caroline ceased her arguments, but as they parted for the night she muttered gloomily that Mary would bitterly regret her decision. Mary wondered whether that was true, but realized that there could be no turning back now. It was too late for that. Mr. Knowle would be with her by the middle of the next morning, and would expect her answer straight away.

They ate breakfast in a somber mood, for Caroline had recognized the futility of further argument, and yet could not bring herself to wish her friend well. Consequently, when Susan appeared and handed Mary a note, apologizing that she had forgotten it earlier, Caroline vented her annoyance on the girl by speaking sharply.

"When did it come?"

"Last night, ma'am, after you'd gone out."

"And you did not give it to us last night? How is that?"

"I'm sorry, ma'am, really I am, but you said not to wait up, and I put it to one side and forgot all about it till this minute!"

Caroline happened to glance at Mary then, and sprang up in alarm.

"Go away," she ordered Susan, and scarcely was the frightened maid out of the room before Caroline was kneeling beside her friend, holding her hand and asking what was amiss.

"You are so pale," she said, when Mary turned bleak eyes towards her. "What is it?"

Mary's color flooded back, and she rose angrily to her feet.

"The fools! The utter fools! Teresa was planning this when she asked for the laudanum, no doubt! To throw us all off the scent for a few hours! She and my precious brother have eloped again, and this is from Matthew!"

She held the note out to Caroline, but before Caroline could take it drew it back and began to read out parts of it.

" 'Teresa is afraid for her life'—well, that is clear, and she has reason to be, but listen to this! 'She thought you her friend, but realizes now that after your treatment of her earlier, when you used physical force to browbeat her at a time when she needed sympathy and tenderness, she can no longer rely on your friendship.' In Heaven's name, what would he have me do when she was in a frenzy of hysteria? I hope he has to deal with her in such a state, and then he'll see how far tenderness will get him!" she said viciously. "Now I understand how it was Sir Ingram was accused of beating her!"

"Thank you," came a suave voice from behind her, and she swung round to find Sir Ingram smiling down at her. "I only wish her other accusations could be disproved so easily!"

"How—how did you get in?" Mary gasped.

"I walked in," he replied calmly. "The maid seemed unwilling to announce me, and so, time being at something of a premium, I declined to stand upon ceremony and announced myself. You have heard, I take it?"

Mary waved the note at him. "From Matthew,"

she explained tersely. "Where will they have gone? Did Teresa leave any indication?"

"She said, most helpfully, that they were taking ship at Bristol with France as their destination. That I take to mean that they are heading for Scotland!"

Caroline gave a sudden choke of laughter. "Then you had best set off after them," she advised. "That is, if you mean to make a push to bring them back?"

"I do," Sir Ingram replied grimly. "I came to ask you, Miss Wyndham, to accompany me, first because I know that you have some influence with both my cousin and your brother, but also because, if we overtake them, it will enable us to protect them from their folly by chaperoning them adequately."

"So now I *have* influence, do I?" Mary demanded furiously. "*Now* I can be used as a chaperone? Do you know, I think I shall wish them good luck! At least Teresa with be free of attacks on her life when she is married and away from Bath!"

So saying, Mary sat down and stared defiantly at Sir Ingram. He took a couple of steps towards her, his look thunderous.

"Heaven preserve me from obstinate women!" he ejaculated. "Are you still nourishing the illusion that I want to murder my cousin for her paltry few thousand? By God, I *could* murder her at times, but not for such a reason, believe me!

She is still in danger, even more so with her marriage intended! The man who wants to be rid of her may even yet be following her, and he'll have a far better prospect of succeeding when she is on a journey, protected only by that mutton-headed brother of yours!"

"You don't seem to have made a very good job of protecting her yourself," Mary retorted, but with a little less conviction in her voice.

"Because I was handicapped by not knowing how it could benefit him, and did not realize one fact. Now I am certain, but if you do not come soon we shall be too late to protect her life or her reputation. Do I have to carry you out to my curricle?"

"I do not understand!" Mary protested weakly, and hastily stood up as he bore down on her, reading the intention of executing his threat clear in his eyes.

"Explanations can wait until we are on the road. Come, they cannot have traveled far overnight. Your servant, Mrs. Grafton. I will restore Miss Wyndham to you as soon as is possible."

So saying, he caught Mary by the hand and almost dragged her from the room. The terrified maid, who had obviously been given orders previously, stood trembling in the hall with Mary's traveling cloak over her arm. Sir Ingram took it with a brief word of thanks, wrapped it round Mary's shoulders, then once again seized her hand and led her to the waiting curricle.

"I will make your apologies to Mr. Knowle," Caroline said gleefully as she watched this departure, but was certain that Mary had not heard her words, and was equally certain that she would not have understood their import if she had.

Without pausing, Sir Ingram bent and picked Mary up to fling her unceremoniously into the curricle. He spoke briefly to his groom and another man waiting there, and then leapt up himself, took the reins, and set off at a fast trot out of the square, threading his way skillfully through the traffic towards Lansdown Hill and the road to the north.

Mary waited, fuming inwardly, until they had a clear stretch of road before them, and then spoke scathingly to Sir Ingram.

"Pray allow me to inform you, Sir Ingram, that you are the most overbearing, the most high-handed, and the most objectionable man it has been my misfortune to meet!"

He glanced briefly at her, laughter in his eyes.

"That sounds decidedly promising," he observed calmly.

"What do you mean?" Mary demanded suspiciously, but he did not reply, and after a moment of silence she asked coldly where they were going.

"Matthew hired a chaise to take them to Gloucester," he explained. "I had sent to make inquiries at all the posting inns, and received the information just now. Previously it had been only a suspicion."

"At what time did they leave?"

"After ten last night, but we cannot be certain as to the exact time. My Aunt Cecy had left Bath earlier that day, and Aunt Hermione thought that Teresa was asleep. She did not see her after she herself retired to bed at ten, and it was morning before her maid raised the alarm. Do not worry, though, for they cannot have traveled very fast in the darkness, so even if they did not stop for the night we should overtake them during the day. The chaise Matthew hired was not the speediest of vehicles, either," he added with a chuckle.

"How do you know that?"

"Well, when I saw your brother the other day, he intimated then that he might remove Teresa from my care. He makes a deplorable schemer, by the way—he is far too honest! So, you see, I had been expecting something of this nature, and had made my plans accordingly. I had—er—arrangements with the appropriate people."

"You mean you bribed them to give Matthew a poor vehicle?" Mary asked bluntly.

Sir Ingram looked at her in amusement. "If you choose so to describe my precautions. I should, incidentally, also have been informed at once, but my bribes, as you would no doubt describe them, do not seem to have been effective. Possibly I gave him too much, for the ostler concerned had imbibed a trifle too freely and was not performing his duties!"

"What do you propose to do when we overtake them? Banish Teresa to one of your country estates?"

"When we overtake them will be the time to determine that. I am concerned first with their safety, rather than preventing this foolish marriage."

"Are they in danger? Do you believe, truly, that someone is making attacks on Teresa?" Mary asked, perplexed. "Who can it be?"

"If it is not myself?" Sir Ingram said, laughing down at her as he passed a laden chaise coming in the opposite direction with barely an inch to spare. "Tell me, did you really suspect that it was I making such ineffectual attempts on her life such as those she described to you when we first met? Come, Miss Wyndham, I do not set out to murder anyone by taking potshots at them or loosening their saddle girths! You will wound my vanity if you admit that you think I could be so inept! When I plan a murder, I will do it far more effectively, I do assure you!"

"Of course I do not believe it," Mary said crossly. "Yet, if there have been attempts on her life, who is it? Who would benefit by Teresa's death?"

"Have you forgotten that whoever it is would have had to dispose of Mrs. Standish too? At least, *I* would have had to before I could have enjoyed Teresa's fortune."

"But she was attacked too, if she really was pushed down the stairs. Yet how could anyone have been in the house? And why kill the parrot?"

"I believe I can guess how she came to fall down the stairs, and how it is connected with the unfortunate bird."

"You may consider that you have solved the mystery, but I am no better informed than I was before!" Mary said crossly.

"My uncle's will was a dangerous one, but he could not be persuaded into altering it," Sir Ingram said reflectively. "Not all Teresa's silliness comes from her mother. He left some capital for Mrs. Standish, from which she could have such income as I determined. When she dies, that capital reverts to Teresa, even if she is then under twenty-five. The rest of his fortune he left in trust for Teresa, again giving me the discretion, along with another trustee, of determining what income she was to enjoy. When she is twenty-five it becomes hers absolutely, but if she dies unmarried before that time, it goes, again freely, to Mrs. Standish."

"So Mrs. Standish would have some capital, and you think that is a motive for murdering Teresa? Surely you cannot suspect her own mother of such wickedness!"

"It has been known," Sir Ingram shrugged, "but

no, I do not believe Aunt Cecy is wicked—merely foolish. She is being used by someone far more dangerous who would expect to gain control of the money were Teresa to die. And naturally Teresa must not marry or this plan would be foiled, for her husband would inherit."

"Then she would be *safe* if she married Matthew!" Mary exclaimed. "So why are you so set against it?"

"I have more than her safety to consider. I will confess that I did not expect their love to endure. I—at first—distrusted love that seemed to arise within a single hour. Teresa's affections have been so volatile hitherto that I did not dare allow her to marry until she had proved more steady." He gave Mary an oddly penetrating glance, but she was staring straight ahead and was unaware of it. "Now I am more convinced of their love, and—I am aware that it is indeed possible to fall suddenly and irrevocably in love."

"Yes, they seem to have done," Mary answered slowly. "Will you then permit the marriage?"

"Let us first disentangle the imbroglio they have fallen into," was all the reply he vouchsafed to that.

10

They made excellent time and, with liberally scattered largesse, the changes of horses were swiftly and efficiently made. When they had been traveling for three hours, Sir Ingram called a brief halt while they drank wine and ate a nuncheon of cold meat and cheese.

"Shall we ever catch up with them?" Mary asked, worried that they had no news of the fugitives.

"They may have traveled all night," he reminded her. "If so, we cannot expect to be near them yet."

The journey, which seemed endless to Mary, continued, and it was several hours later before they had news that a couple answering to the description Sir Ingram had given had passed through and changed horses an hour before.

"There were a proper commotion," the ostler said slowly, grinning at the recollection. "The young gent wanted to stay 'ere for 'is dinner, but the young lady would not, saying that she would go on by 'erself if 'e insisted, and so, arter a big argy-bargy, they both went on. She wanted to change the carriage too, for it were nearly fallin' apart, but there wasn't none 'ere, and she 'ad to make do."

"We shall soon be upon them," Sir Ingram said with satisfaction, gathering up the reins and preparing to move off, when Mary clutched at his arm and cried:

"It can't be! There, in that window to the left, Mrs. Standish! Oh, she's seen me looking and moved away. But why is she here? She is staying with friends!"

"This is an unexpected piece of good fortune. You had best remain here," Sir Ingram flung over his shoulder as he leapt down from the curricle and strode into the inn. Mary, disregarding his orders and determined not to be left out of this, jumped down from the curricle and ran after him.

The landlord approached, bowing obsequiously and rubbing his fat hands together.

"And what may I do for you, sir?"

Sir Ingram was explaining the location of the room where Mary had seen Mrs. Standish at the window.

"We believe it is a friend of ours, but we caught only a glimpse of the lady's face," he continued.

"A Mrs. Standish," Mary added.

The landlord looked puzzled. "I have no one of that name here at present," he apologized, looking distressed that it was beyond his powers to conjure up such a person.

"But I was certain!" Mary exclaimed, and Sir Ingram smiled with grim satisfaction.

"Oh, then no doubt it is our friend's sister, they are very alike. A Mrs. Morris," he suggested suavely, grasping Mary's hand in his and giving it a warning squeeze.

"Mrs. Morris? Oh, yes, indeed! The lady came late last night with her husband," the landlord informed them, relieved that the mystery had been satisfactorily explained.

"Is Mr. Morris here now?"

"No. He had to ride out for a short while, he said, not above an hour since."

Sir Ingram whirled about and ran out of the inn, dragging Mary with him. He picked her up and threw her into the curricle, leapt up himself, and set the horses in motion, almost knocking the ostler that held the reins off his feet. Before Mary had recovered her breath he had swung the curricle recklessly through the entrance to the inn yard, and was threading his way rapidly and hazardously through the traffic that thronged the main street of the little town.

"What in the world? How did you know that they were married?" Mary demanded when they were once more safely on an almost empty road.

"I did not, but I surmised it. The provisions of my uncle's will made it likely that some villain would think to gain the money by marrying Aunt Cecy and killing Teresa. Morris must have persuaded Aunt Cecy to keep their marriage a secret to throw off suspicion. He had the opportunities needed to attack Teresa, but he made his mistake when he killed the parrot."

"I can scarce credit it! Rodney Morris! He is nought but a foppish dandy!"

"He apes the dandy, but you have seen him on a horse. He is much more than he pretends. Did you never suspect him, even in the caves?"

"How did he contrive that?"

"He took Teresa's hand, as she told us, in the darkness. Only she thought it was Matthew, for he was also near her. He must have felled the guide and then led Teresa down that small passage. He had been in the caves before, you see, and could have known of that precipice. When I heard her scream I went after them, and as I reached her I felt someone slip past me in the darkness. When the light was brought he was found solicitously bending over the guide, but I knew then who it must have been."

"You pretended it had been her imagination."

"I dared not alarm her, for I needed better proof. The parrot provided me with that."

"How? What has the parrot to do with it?"

"That proved that someone was in the house secretly. Who more likely than Aunt Cecy's husband, visiting her when the rest of the family were out? I suspect that Aunt Cecy had just let him in, or was about to let him out, when the parrot made a noise and caused her to lose her step, hence that fall, and, in his rage at near-discovery, Morris killed it. Or the parrot might have learned some incriminating phrase and had to be disposed of."

Fleetingly Mary recalled the bird's display on the night of the party. She nodded slowly.

"And now he has followed them. Oh, do hurry!"

"He is an opportunist. He could not have planned the attack in the caves, but he must have taken advantage of the fact that they reached that spot, in near-darkness, with Teresa beside him. Now he has seized another opportunity and followed them. It must have been a surprise to him to see them here. I had not expected him to have come with Aunt Cecy, but thought rather that he would have followed them from Bath."

They raced along for a while, Sir Ingram feathering corners expertly and overtaking all the slower vehicles on the road. After covering several miles, Sir Ingram exclaimed with satisfaction and pointed with his whip. Some distance in front of them a post chaise had overturned and come to rest in the ditch at the side of the road. As they drew nearer they could see that it was deserted and that a near-side wheel lay a few yards behind the vehicle.

"They will have sought the nearest inn, and as we have not lately passed one, they will have gone forward," Sir Ingram remarked, sweeping past the wreckage of the chaise.

Sure enough, within half a mile they saw a small hostelry, little more than an alehouse, set back amongst the trees. Sir Ingram drew up outside the front door and jumped down, turning to give Mary a hand. She sprang lightly down just as an ancient ostler limped wearily round the corner of the building.

"We be uncommon busy today," he muttered, but took the reins and led the steaming horses away.

Sir Ingram gave Mary an encouraging smile, but she was so concerned at what they might find, either as a result of the accident or from the machinations of Mr. Morris, that she simply returned the glance with a mute appeal.

Inside the inn the landlord was frantically shouting instructions to his underlings, a clumsy-looking youth and a slatternly girl. He turned to greet the newcomers, pushing his none too clean hands through his lank, greasy hair. The grimace he achieved was far from welcoming.

"Have a young lady and a gentleman arrived here from a wrecked chaise?" Sir Ingram demanded.

The landlord glowered at them.

"Aye."

"Are they hurt?" Mary asked anxiously.

"They can both still walk," was the ungracious reply.

"They are our young relatives. We were following and came upon the wreckage. Pray take us to them."

Reluctantly the landlord moved forwards.

"I've only two rooms, and they've taken both, and we're not used to providing dinner for the quality," he jerked out as he began to climb the somewhat rickety stairs.

"You need not disturb yourself, fellow. We would be grateful for whatever you can provide, and then if there is a larger inn nearby we will settle what we owe for these rooms and remove to it."

At the prospect of getting rid of his visitors while still receiving payment, his countenance brightened, and he looked with a much friendlier air at Sir Ingram.

"You must be traveling strung out," he commented. "First the young uns, then the fellow what says he's her father, and now you. Them's the rooms."

He nodded along the landing and stood aside to let them pass. Voices came from the further room, and Sir Ingram went straight to it and lifted the latch, but the door was bolted on the inside. Unhesitatingly he put his shoulder to it and the flimsy structure gave way immediately, the sound of splintering wood mingling with an astonished protest from the landlord.

Beyond Sir Ingram, Mary caught a glimpse of Teresa's startled face, and then he stepped further inside the room and she could see into it. She had time to notice only that the three of them—Rodney Morris, Teresa, and Matthew—were seated round a small table, before Mr. Morris sprang to his feet with an oath and reached for his cane, which lay on the table. He twisted it and pulled, and the innocent cane became a wickedly sharp-pointed swordstick, which he leveled at Sir Ingram.

Teresa screamed and clung to Matthew. Mr. Morris looked round.

"Oh, dear, I was quite convinced that we had been invaded by ruffians," he murmured gently. "Dear boy, do you normally enter a room in such an alarming fashion? Could you not knock and wait for the door to be opened?"

"I do not take chances," Sir Ingram answered grimly. "Not with murderers. Wyndham, pray keep the ladies well out of the way."

Mr. Morris did not lower his sword, but kept it

pointed steadily at Sir Ingram. The others drew back into a corner behind the table.

"Are you deranged? What is this nonsense?"

"No nonsense. I have proof that will send you to the gallows on a charge of attempted murder of your stepdaughter. You need not trouble to deny it, for I have seen your wife and the evidence will hang you."

Suddenly Mr. Morris sprang forward, aiming his sword for Sir Ingram's throat. Sir Ingram leapt to one side, seized a small stool, and twisted it before him, so that the next thrust of the sword was foiled by it, and before Mr. Morris could draw back, his sword had been forced from his hand and fell to the floor. Sir Ingram kicked it aside, flung away the stool, and faced Mr. Morris, who was aiming punches at him in what Matthew, somewhat astonished, realized was a far from amateur fashion. Sir Ingram was, however, a more skillful master of the art, and evaded the blows meant for him. He feinted with his left, and then, so swiftly that the watchers hardly saw what he did, he delivered a punch with his right fist that connected squarely with Mr. Morris's chin and sent him staggering across the room to collapse groaning against the wall beneath the small window.

Sir Ingram inspected him cursorily, then bent to retrieve the sword and laid it on the table.

"My, that were as neat a wisty castor as ever

I've seen!" the landlord exclaimed, his dismay at these untoward doings submerged in his admiration of Sir Ingram's expertise.

Sir Ingram glanced at him.

"I will pay for any damage," he said briefly. "Can you hasten dinner for us?"

The landlord, his former surliness vanished, made haste to do as he was bid, and Sir Ingram turned back to the others.

"I beg your pardon, ladies, but it was unavoidable. I do not think he will trouble us much now."

Teresa, who had remained clasped in Matthew's arms, continued to sob unrestrainedly, while Matthew looked at Sir Ingram and his sister.

"How did you find us? And what are you doing here, Mary?"

"Your sister has most kindly come to lend you countenance," Sir Ingram explained smoothly. "We can all return to Bath in the morning, where we can discuss your future calmly. You are in no more danger, Teresa, so do, I beg you, cease these lamentations! It is this contemptible worm who was attacking you, not I, and he is powerless to do so any longer!"

"It is a trick," Teresa declared, staring fiercely at her cousin. She indicated the still recumbent Mr. Morris. "*He* tried to trick us into going back with him, saying that he would obtain your permission for our marriage. As if he could have changed your mind," she added scornfully.

"What was that about his wife?" Matthew suddenly remembered.

Sir Ingram smiled. "Oh, he has for some time been secretly married to Mrs. Standish. I suppose we ought to say Mrs. Morris now."

Teresa stared at him. "What did you say? He and Mama? And Mama has been scolding *me* for trying to make what she called a clandestine marriage! Oh, this is beyond everything!"

"I agree that it was not the most felicitous example to set you," her cousin said quietly. "He hoped, by killing you, to get control of your fortune through his wife. His first attempts were arranged to appear as accidents, but when none of them succeeded he grew desperate, knowing that he had very little time before you married. Hence the attack in the cave." He explained what he had told Mary. "It was he, also, who killed the parrot when he visited your mother."

"With his swordstick!" Matthew exclaimed, revolted. "But why do such a grisly thing to a harmless bird!"

"Not so harmless if his noise, or an incriminating phrase he had picked up, would betray Morris."

"I am not going back with either you or him!" Teresa suddenly declared. "I don't know which of you is telling the truth, and I am not going with *anyone* except Matthew, and I *shall* marry him, and you will not stop me, and you will not marry me yourself, Ingram!"

"Have you any more money than the last time you eloped?" was all the reply he deigned to give to this challenge.

"Yes!" she retorted. "Matthew still has some he won at cards, and I have sold my pearls! Mama gave me that notion!"

"I might have expected that," Sir Ingram commented. "You must be very weary after such a long and tiresome journey, so we will discuss it after we have dined."

There was a scraping sound behind them, and, suddenly recalling the recumbent form of Mr. Morris, they swung round to see that he had recovered his senses and had quietly raised himself by pulling on the windowsill. The noise was of his boot scraping on the sill as he began to clamber out of the window. A couple of feet away the branch of an oak tree was visible, and as Sir Ingram sprang across the room in an attempt to seize Mr. Morris, he swung himself fully out of the window and grasped this branch.

For a few seconds his hands clung to it, but as it bent under his weight he gave a cry of terror, and his hands slipped gradually, slowly, until the branch, too weak to take the strain, fractured, and Rodney Morris plummeted down to fall with a sickening thud on the cobbled path below that led round this side of the inn towards the stables.

Sir Ingram gazed down at him for a moment, and then turned to run down that staircase and out of the front door. By the time he reached Morris the landlord and the ostler were already there, and Mary, following close behind him, saw them shake their heads dolefully.

They made way for Sir Ingram to kneel beside Mr. Morris, but a rapid examination showed him that there was no chance that the man could be alive, for the side of his head was crushed where he had struck it against the cobblestones.

"Can you find somewhere for him to be laid?" Sir Ingram asked, and the landlord, speechless, nodded. Sir Ingram turned to take Mary's arm and lead her from the scene.

"It must be better this way," he said gently. "Whether my Aunt Cecy loved him or no, she could not have borne the knowledge that her husband had attempted to murder her daughter. Now there need be no fuss and no scandal. Truly it is better for all of us, even Morris, horrible though his death was."

"It was so sudden," Mary whispered, and she shuddered. He felt her sway slightly and led her to a bench set beside the door of the inn where he persuaded her to sit down, talking soothingly until she was calmer.

"Thank you, I am better now," she said after a while and rose to go back inside the inn. "I ought to go to Teresa."

They went back upstairs, but the room they had left so precipitously was empty. The door of the other room that had been for their use was wide open, and Mary went in, but it too was empty, and there was no baggage or other indication that the room had been occupied.

This room looked out over the back of the inn, and Mary crossed to look through the window. Below her, Sir Ingram's curricle was being driven away from the stables by Matthew, and at that moment Teresa, seated in it, turned round and saw Mary at the window.

"Quickly!" Mary heard her exclaim, and Matthew whipped up the horse.

There was a low chuckle from behind her, and Mary swung round in dismay.

"Hurry, you must go after them! There is the horse Mr. Morris rode, you could take that!"

He smiled and shook his head. "And leave you here, alone with that unprepossessing landlord, to explain a violent death to the magistrate, who is, I have no doubt, being summoned here at this very minute? You cannot have a very good opinion of me."

"Oh, I do not care for that! Obtain another carriage, then! We must follow them!"

"Have you so great an objection to your brother marrying my cousin?"

She stared at him, nonplussed. "But you do!"

"She is safe now, and I have ceased to care what she does. If Matthew is prepared to take her with all her wildness and mad pranks, then he is welcome to the unenviable task of taking care of her!"

"But—but—a clandestine wedding!"

"They are welcome to that also, and I have the strong notion that Teresa would feel deprived of a privilege if she were forced to have a conventional bridal! Let them go, and we can think about ourselves. It is too late to make arrangements for traveling back to Bath tonight, I fear."

"Oh, dear, I completely forgot!" Mary exclaimed remorsefully. "How very dreadful of me!"

"You forgot?"

"Yes, an—an appointment! The fact is," she explained in confusion as he remained staring at her, his eyebrows raised, an enigmatic smile on his lips, "Mr. Knowle was coming to—to visit me."

Sir Ingram laughed. "Poor man, to discover his bird flown! Will he reject you utterly when he discovers that you have spent the night alone at an inn with me? I would imagine him to have very strong views on the propriety of the behavior of the woman he wished to marry."

"I suppose I need not tell him everything," Mary said slowly, "and there has certainly been no impropriety! But how very dreadful of me to have forgotten him! I was so concerned for Teresa."

"I am sure such a correct man would not understand, and might not wish to be connected by marriage to such a disreputable family," Sir Ingram said solemnly. "I can see that, having utterly ruined your reputation, and with it the chances of so estimable a marriage, I shall have to make amends by offering for you myself!"

Mary stared at him, and slowly a blush suffused her cheeks.

"Do not be so ridiculous!" she managed to say, and turned away from him to hide her burning cheeks. "You have no call to make such a sacrifice!" she added in tight voice.

He took her hand in his, tightening his clasp when she would have freed it, and turned her to face him. With an immense effort she forced herself to look up into his face, and encountered a most disturbing smile.

"Why in the world should you imagine it to be a sacrifice, foolish one? It is what I have intended since the moment I saw you, my love! My previous attempt to speak to you was frustrated by that abominable cousin of mine yesterday morning, if you recall. I am hoping that you will not feel constrained to accept me now because of our compromising situation, but because it is what you wish yourself. Can it be so, Mary my love?"

"You are merely being polite," she whispered, her heart beating uncomfortably fast. "There is no need, truly!"

"Now it is you that is ridiculous, my sweet," he said gently. "Have you accepted Mr. Knowle? If you have, you can always say that you were mistaken."

"No, but I promised to give him an answer today! What will he have thought of me?" she said distractedly.

"What would that answer have been?" he insisted, taking her chin in his hand and tilting her face up so that she was forced to look at him.

"I was going to accept," she admitted slowly.

"Is it possible that you love him?" he asked swiftly, his eyes narrowing.

"No, but—well, he said that it was wrong to love before marriage, and that it would come, and besides—"

"He is a dolt, or worse. And besides what?" he demanded, taking his hand from her face and slipping it about her waist to draw her close to him.

"I—my father wishes to return to Oxford, and he had the impression that I was about to marry," she said reluctantly, trembling within his embrace and bending her head to escape his intent gaze. "I could not disappoint him, for he was so looking forward to settling there!"

Suddenly he laughed. "That was because I told him," he said calmly.

She looked up at him then, startled. "You told him? I do not understand!"

"Those two days I was away from Bath I visited him in Oxford and obtained his blessing."

"That is where you were," she exclaimed. "But how could you be so certain I would accept? What did you tell my father?"

"I read the look in your eyes and I had hopes. I may have misled your father a trifle, but my hopes were near certainty. So you see, my darling, I can prove to you that I am not asking you merely because we are alone here, but because I have always intended to, since the moment I walked into your drawing room and found you defending Teresa so valiantly! It was then that I understood how it was possible for two apparently rational people to succumb to a passion so overwhelming that nothing else mattered. I hope Teresa and Matthew are truly in love, as I am and as I believe you are. But tell me, can you feel any love for me?"

Mary took a deep breath, but it did not dispel the elation in her whole being. She smiled at him tremulously, her eyes shining.

"I—I have not dared to admit it, even to myself! I did not know! I *wanted* to believe that you were what you seemed, but Teresa was so very convincing, I did not know what to believe!"

He drew her firmly into his arms and kissed her, lingeringly, gently, until shyly she responded.

"Foolish one, to believe one jot of her wild imaginings! Well, before you commit yourself irrevocably, I will have to rebut them!"

Ignoring Mary's protests that she did not believe what Teresa had accused him of, he sat on a chair and pulled her onto his knee, holding her closely to him.

"I suppose she told you that I had murdered Delaine? In reality he died in a brothel brawl, but Teresa would not allow that to be true of her current idol. Also she holds it against me that I dismissed her old governess. Matty begged me to find someone better able to control Teresa, which I failed to do, incidentally, and I gave her a pension and a cottage to which she thankfully retired. What else? Oh, the beatings, and the refusal to allow her complete freedom. I collect you have seen her in an hysterical tantrum?"

Mary chuckled, relaxing confidingly in his arms. "Yes, and beaten her myself, *and* felt tempted to lock her in her room with only bread and water," she confessed.

"As for wanting to marry her, can you really think me so lacking in common sense, not to mention self-preservation?"

Mary shook her head, her eyes full of laughter, and he exclaimed wordlessly, pulling her head down so that he could kiss her again, and this time she returned his kisses more confidently.

"Do you love me, my darling beloved one?" he asked eventually.

"I'd appear an abandoned wretch indeed if I said no in this situation," she said, laughing and avoiding his questing lips. "Yes, my dear, I do, though I've only just realized it—or admitted it to myself!"

"Then I ought to have done this weeks ago! When will you be my wife?"

She gazed at him, amusement in her glance. "There is just one other accusation," she said demurely. "I did not *precisely* understand the reference, naturally, but Teresa mentioned something called Haymarket-ware. I always thought one bought hay there?"

He grinned, no whit abashed, and kissed her until she was breathless.

"You are a minx, and I've a mind to roll you in the hay!" he threatened, then his tone became serious. "You need fear no competition for my favors, for I am utterly and completely yours for ever, my one true love," he averred.

A long time afterwards a discreet cough and a tap at the door aroused them again to an awareness of their surroundings.

"Dinner is ready, sir, and I'm afraid the other young lady and gentleman have gone off in your curricle. My ostler has only just discovered it, him having been so busy, so to speak!"

can replace the curricle. I should have been really offended had they been my own cattle! Well, landlord, in that case we had best use their rooms instead. Bring your best wine—we have something to celebrate!"

Shaking his head at the inexplicable behavior of the quality, the landlord went gloomily away, and Sir Ingram turned, opening his arms wide for Mary, who had retreated in some confusion to the window when they had been disturbed.

"Would you prefer to follow them to Scotland after all, for our own wedding?" he asked. "I do not mean to be kept waiting for long, I warn you!"

She laughed. "I will not do so, but I am proud and happy to be marrying you, and want our friends to share our joy."

"Then we had best dine and be ready to set off early tomorrow. I cannot be content until you are mine."

He crushed her to him, and this time the landlord, heading a procession of menials bearing the offerings from his kitchen, had to knock several times before he was invited to enter the room and spread out the feast.